Lock Down Publications and Ca$h Presents

CRIME
PAYS

It Comes at A Cost

I0658208

By
Self Made Tay

First Edition 2025

Printed in the United States of America

Lock Down Publications
P.O. Box 944
Stockbridge, GA 30281
www.lockdownpublications.com

Like our page on Facebook: Lock Down Publications
www.facebook.com/lockdownpublications.ldp

Contact Information
FB: Imade Tay 2xs
IG: SelfMadeTay123 or SelfMadeTay33
Email: selfmadetay33@gmail.com
YouTube: Youtube.com/@selfmadetay33
More information on books:
www.amazon.com/author/selfmadetay26

Stay Connected with Us!

Text **LOCKDOWN** to 22828 to stay up-to-date with new releases, sneak peaks, contests and more…

Like our page on Facebook:
Lock Down Publications

Join Lock Down Publications/The New Era Reading Group

Visit our website:
www.lockdownpublications.com

Follow us on Instagram:
Lock Down Publications

Email Us: We want to hear from you!

Acknowledgements/Shoutouts

To my family and fans, I appreciate the continued support. Your patience truly inspires me. It motivates me to create stories that not only entertain but also offer valuable insights or challenges for the audience. I am committed to maintaining consistent progress and further developing my abilities through each challenge encountered. My gratitude is gracefully with you genuinely. Thank you!

I want to extend my sincere appreciation to my wife and children for their unwavering support and patience as I devoted countless hours to master my craft with these stories. The time you guys sacrificed will never go unnoticed, promise. As we progress through this journey, which I am confident will yield positive results, it is important to appreciate each moment along the way. I Love y'all! #TayGang #TeamJohnson

To my new readers; welcome, you're in for a ride. Thanks for joining us on this journey! Now let's get into the story of **Crime Pays: Lesson 3.** Remember, **It Comes At a Cost.** LDP's, Self Made Tay.

Lesson 3.1
It'll Come a Time for War...

Mac leaned back in the chair, eyes steady on Keem. "You know very well that this is what comes with this type of lifestyle." Keem paced the empty floor of Club Jungle, the bass from the speakers rumbled at a low vibration. Aside from the presence of Mac and Keem, there were a few employees preparing for the opening later tonight. There were a couple half full glasses of spirits resting on top of the bar. Thick smoke clouds of weed hung in the air. Mac suggested weed and alcohol to settle Keem some. None of it touched Keem's mood though. His mind was somewhere darker as he and Mac discussed the few scraps of beef that threatened the flow of money they'd been making.

"I know that you want to go at this situation on your own. Show your face and remind your opposers. And even yourself, what comes behind fucking with a man like you. But if you move too fast, especially without putting the proper thought into your judgement, shit is liable to get sloppy. Since you're aware of how sloppiness can affect your focus and planning, I strongly suggest you manage your emotions and reconsider your approach."

Keem knew that Mac was right. He usually was. Usually, it never bothered Keem. But this time it did. His emotions were pushing Keem's tactical shrewdness to the back of his mind, throwing him off his game, which was a rarity. Luckily, for Keem, he had a man like Mac in his corner.

"It is also certain that you know, in this game, there will inevitably be a time for war. Going off the story you just ran

5

down to me, now is one of them times. Over the years, I have come to learn that the best way to win a war is to keep it under your control. And one of the best ways to do that is perfect timing. Move on your time, retaliate on your time, stop whatever whenever but, on your time! The last thing you would want anybody to do, especially an enemy, is for them to know that you're coming. For them or anyone else for that matter to know your upcoming moves. You don't think that those fuckers are gearing up preparing for your arrival? If they were smart, they would be."

"I know they are." Keem's hands were crossed behind his back as his feet still went back and forth across the marble floor.

"Exactly!" Mac said. "So, you know this for sure. Yet, you're sitting right here telling me that you're about to run right into an ambush like a chicken with its head cut off running into traffic. You're not thinking clearly at all. This is not the Keem I molded. The Keem I met, maybe. But this is not the man that you've grown into. I don't know what it's going to take, but you need to get out of your fucking feelings so you can begin to strategize and get these roaches out of the kitchen. So, we can get back to eating and continue on with our business at hand."

Mac was beginning to show a few signs of frustration. Since he was one who always seemed to keep his cool even under tons of pressure, it looked worse than what it really was. "You said that other than your little brother, Shy, that no one was hurt. He'll be okay. Don't worry about that. You also said that you were able to get rid of two of the men that blitzed you, right? Sounds like right here, right now, you are perfectly fine. So, for now, I simply suggest that you go find you a bitch, dip your dick in some pussy, go to the spa, grab you a massage, go count some money, or do whatever it is that'll put your mind at ease. I promise you, once you're calm, the most brilliant plot will come to your mind as if you were Sun Tzu himself. And while you're waiting for that brainstorm to happen, I have a little something that may help a lot with your situation."

Mac picked up a card from off the table, waited for Keem to walk past him for the hundredth time, and handed him the card. "It's a contact. His name's Spook."

"Spook?" Keem stopped in his tracks staring at the card with confusion.

"Yes. Something that is just as good as controlling the war with your timing is having a pair of neutral hands. It wouldn't hurt to consider it. Besides, it stirs things up when you use the element of surprise."

"Alright, I get you. Say less."

"At least consider it." After that, Mac fished out ten thousand dollars that was hidden in the arm rest of his recliner chair. "Give this to little brother for me." He handed the cash to Keem. "Shy is a strong man, Keem. All around the board. He's been sharp on all his edges for a while now. Especially considering his age, unlike you were. You can't expect him to come out like you, live up to your expectations, or do things the way you've done them."

"I know. That's not what I even want for him."

"And I understand that. But just because he won't do things the way you've done them, doesn't mean he won't fall into the lifestyle you choose. My best advice is to let him make his own decision and guide him in the best way you can down whatever road he chooses. Trust me, the worst thing you could do is force someone into doing something. Motherfuckers so stubborn, that even if they want to do the very thing that you're forcing them to do, they'll buck against it with rebellion. Not only is Shy strong. He's also smart and talented. Trust him and have faith that he'll walk in the right direction. If you continue to force him, it'll only confuse and blind him. Now get your emotional ass out of my spot! With all of them soft ass feeling. Fucking up my energy and shit like that. Feel like that shit starting to rub off on me right now." Mac made sure that he threw in a touch of humor with his words. But that didn't take away from the fact that he was dead ass serious.

"Alright, bossman. You got it." Keem walked over to Mac to shake the man's hand.

"Oh, I know I got it, young buck. Get your shit together. So, you can have it too. All this shit is going to come out in your favor. But only if you play your cards the right way. Now go handle your business like I know you would."

"I'm on it, boss. I'll get up with you soon." Keem excited the apartment with only one thing on his mind other than his brother. And that was murder.

Lesson 3.2
Be Ready

A knock came at the door of the YNT hangout. BM whipped the gun off his hip and quickly placed an index finger up to his lips. "Shhhh…"

Ever since that shootout with the Da Fam, BM and the rest of the YNT members have been extra cautious about the way they have been moving recently. Pistol in hand, BM crept to the front door like a tiger. Just as he approached the door, another set of knocks came rapping at the door. "Who the fuck is it?"

"Who the fuck you think it is?" was the reply from the other side. "Open the mother fucking door, nigga. Before a motherfucker catch a nigga lacking out this bitch."

"Oh, them must be the tools," Bank assumed, recognizing the voice of the person knocking on the door.

"Better be," Shoota hoped with a demanding force. "It's about fucking time, shit."

"Oh, it ain't nobody but Tru soft ass." BM opened the door with the gun at a forty-five-degree angle still on ten.

"Maine, open the door and get out the damn way. Nigga always talking shit. Look like you are the soft one. What, you scared to open the door or something? We have to come up with a secret door knock or some. Plus, I just text y'all nigga and told y'all I was on the way."

"Quit bitching, nigga." BM closed and locked the door. But not before taking a quick look up and down the hallway. Making sure it was clear. "Yo ass in this bitch now. You keep talking shit, I'ma throw yo ass out and let the opps have your ass. See if you talk all that shit to them how you do to the gang."

"Nigga, you already know—"

"Shut the fuck up!" BM gave Tru a smack to the back of the head. It was not too heavy of a strike, but it was not light either. "Nigga still fucking talking after I just told his ass to shut the hell up." BM looked up at the rest of the members that were looking at the interaction. "Do you have the shit with you?" Looking up from Tru, BM laid his eyes on Shoota who held a slight smugly smile upon his face. "This nigga," he mumbled.

"Of course. I told y'all niggas the shit was going to work. I even came up on extra shit while on the mission." Tru took a few steps, heading towards the middle of the living room floor, carrying three bags in total. One in each hand, one on his back. Dropping the two in his grip to free up his hands, he then pulled the other bag off his back. He unzipped the bookbag and slowly dumped the contents onto the carpet.

"Most of these motherfuckers pistols, except for this mother fucker right here." As he spoke, Tru lifted a SIG MCX Rattler Canebrake. "This joint right here—this bitch shoot AR bullets. They say this one of the smallest assault rifles out."

Tru didn't get the chance to finish his sentence before BM cut him off and snatched the gun right from his hands.

"Okay, Tru, I see you coming through for the gang. What else you got in that mother fucker? I gotta make sure you really got some good shit in these bags before I give you your props."

On the low, Tru was already getting irritated with the gang. "Shit, I'm trying to show your ass if you let me."

Tru's words were slightly underneath his breath. Being that BM was already right next to him—and with the apartment quiet—he heard every word. Tru tried to play it off and go right along with what he had aimed to do before the interruption. To be honest, he wanted to say a whole lot more than just that but was glad he didn't.

The tension between BM and Tru had been at a steady climb in recent weeks. Although Tru had the least bit of idea as to why, in the back of BM's mind he lost a little more respect for Tru with each day that passed. If you knew anything about BM, then you knew he should be the last to judge. Yet he did so anyway. And to him, Tru was just a disloyal, stupid son of a bitch.

Even though BM knew that Tru was unaware of the fact that BM was the one who not only shot his cousin E but was also the one that put him in jail, BM still looked at Tru as if he was a certified traitor. It was a reflective mirror that BM looked at, and it was himself that he saw in others.

One thing he knew for sure was that E was not dead, and one day he might be exposed as E's attempted murderer. *Whose side would Tru take when that time came?* BM always thought to himself.

If he didn't pick YNT, he would be a dangerous enemy due to the information he knew. But if he didn't go against the grain of the gang and decided to hang around, BM would still frown upon him. Tru was in a lose/lose situation and wasn't even aware of it.

"Alright, anyway," Tru tried to continue, hoping that he wouldn't be rudely interrupted again. For some reason, in his mind, he thought he should have been a little more privileged over the rest of his peers when it came to BM—simply because he was E's little cousin and BM had watched him grow up from pampers.

"If y'all niggas are paying any attention, as you can see, we got all kinds of handguns—mostly Glocks, though. Y'all niggas know that's a lock for them mother fuckers. That way, when it comes time to lay any of them niggas down and we must throw the straps, we'll already have some backup to throw on our hips."

Tru unzipped another section of the bookbag, pulling out two hands full of boxes.

"Of course, we got some shit of nails to go with the tools," he said, full of pride, showing off the boxes of bullets by holding them up in the air as if they were stacks of money fresh out of the bank. "Just like the boss ordered. But that's small work. Over here…"

Tru shifted over to one of the bigger bags that he held when he walked through the door. If he didn't have everyone's attention at first, he surely had it now.

"This pretty mother fucker right here is an AAC Honey Badger, for y'all rookie-ass niggas that don't know," he announced after unzipping the bag and pulling out the first assault rifle, he got his hands on. "Her ass spits out .300 AAC Blackouts."

"You mean 7.62s?" Shoota inquired, implying correction. "Why you gotta be so complicated?"

"'Cause, nigga, the shit just sounds better," Tru shot back. "Of course, we got a couple AR-15s and some ARCs. They shoot the same type of bullets. So does this AR-18. It's only one of these bitches. Next, we have this bad mother fucker. The Russians named her ADS—she's a member of the Bullpup family and is specialized for underwater combat."

"Nigga, which one of us your ass think is gon' be shooting underneath water and shit? We live in a concrete jungle. Ain't no mother fucking water around here," one of the members questioned before making the obvious statement and receiving a handful of laughs.

"Shidd, you never know." That was Tru's comeback.

As he moved on to showcasing the remaining luggage of artillery, the weapons he revealed were AG-043s, HKs, AKs, and of course, the city's favorite baby rifle—the Draco—amongst a couple of other assault rifles. In addition to the other weapons Tru displayed, there were a handful of shotgun pumps.

"Okay, I see you went out and came back with the works," BM complimented. "I guess you ain't all talk after all. That's what's up. Now we really ready for these niggas. But on the real though, I don't think we have to trip too much. We just gon' stick to our regular shit and keep chasing these bands.

"We've got the chance to get the most money we ever got in our lives. All of us. As a matter of fact, we about to get more money than them niggas done ever got. They think they the top niggas in the game, but that was before we came into this game with the determination for domination that we have.

"But just in case niggas do want to get to tripping and shit like that," BM cocked one of the assault rifles and examined it, "we'll most definitely have something waiting for their asses—at the front and back door."

Lesson 3.3
The Value of Freedom

"What's up, fool? Tell me you got some good news." Flex was laid back on the bottom bunk, reading one of the latest books from Lockdown Publications. "You wasn't even down that bitch that long for real." He sat up on the bunk and laid the book to his side. Looking at E, Flex tried to see if he could catch a hint of what went on with the meeting judging off E's demeanor.

The cell door slammed behind E, and he walked over to the small table attached to the wall, taking a seat on top of it.

"Shawty sounds like she knows what the fuck she is talking about. She's talking like she's about to tear this case apart."

E had just returned from a visit with his lawyer, Dawn Mornings. A woman that was an up-and-coming lawyer on the scene. So far, she had beaten most of her cases at an eighty-one percent win rate—and when she didn't, she still made sure her clients came out on top with a solid plea agreement. E heard about her through Flex. She was the same one who helped him out with his case. How Flex got blessed enough to even know her was another story altogether.

"So, she ain't talking about a plea deal or nothing?" Flex pressed, wanting more details.

"Hell naw! She's talking like we gone beat this shit, for shit sure."

"I told you, nigga," Flex gloated, proudly. Regardless of people's opinion about Flex, the last thing he wanted was to see a nigga go through the system of incarceration. It made him happy knowing that E had a fighting opportunity to regain his freedom in such a short time—especially since Flex gave a helping hand in guaranteeing E that opportunity to do so.

"Shawty ass a beast. You got court in about another week. Your ass about to be up out this bitch, fool. Them twelve bands you paid shawty about to pay off. If I was you, I'll be happy as a motherfucker."

"Shidd . . . I do feel confident. But I'ma stay humble until we see what's really gone happen. Don't act like you don't know how them court rooms are. I'll believe her ass when I see it."

"Nigga, you gon' be good. For one, you're really a good nigga. I know sometimes it seem like the good niggas got it the hardest, but shit be playin' out certain ways for a reason. Like, for instance—you did get towed off on some fuck shit—but you came in this bitch, snatched you up a bad bitch, linked in with a real official nigga like me, and I know for a fact you gotta be over fifty bands up off them strips by now."

"Shidd, fifty? Nigga, I'm damn near pushin' a hundred," E clarified, not bragging just saying facts.

"Exactly, nigga! It wasn't no humbug why you fell in here. Everything happens for a reason, my nigga. Now get your ass ready to hit them streets so I can take over in this bitch with them strips and shit. Run me up a couple hundred thousand before this well run dry."

E laughed Flex off a little, knowing he was right. The laugh was a grateful one—thankful to have a solid nigga like Flex in his corner, especially after losing his best friend of decades.

"Naw, dead ass though, you on point with your words. You done put a nigga on game about a lotta shit. I'ma go out here and fuck these streets up. Niggas ain't gon' know what hit they ass—or where it's comin' from, for that matter. Yeah though, we gon' know for sure what the move gon' be next week. If everything goes right, then you already know I got you, nigga. You ain't gon' have to worry 'bout shit. You feel me?"

"Say less, nigga. I just want you to stay fuckin' free and do what you need to do. Everything after that just extra, for real."

"Already, I got you, fool."

E flopped down onto the floor where his mat broke his fall and pulled the blanket over his head, waiting for the cell doors to pop open.

Lesson 3.4
Money Can Buy Happiness

"Baby, I know what I'm doing."

Shawndra giggled at Derek, who had his arms wrapped around hers, helping her paint the walls. The two of them were doing whatever they could with their own hands before it was time to bring in real help for the serious renovations. They had just bought a run-down house on the Church Hill side of Richmond City. Working as hard as they had put them a little ahead of the schedule they'd planned for themselves.

"I know you know," Derek replied with a slight chuckle. "I just needed a good enough reason to get behind all this ass you carryin' around with you."

The honesty made Shawndra laugh. She gave Derek a playful tap on the side of his thigh as he gently caressed her from behind, both of them stroking the paint roller up and down the wall.

"You know damn well my ass ain't that phat. And you don't need any excuse to love on what's yours. Please, baby—by all means, be my guest."

Derek took a palm full of her left ass cheek and massaged it with a soft, loving touch.

"Your wish is my command. Trust me, baby, the pleasure all mine."

For a moment, Shawndra was speechless. She felt lucky to have found love like this. The energy between them was high, and words weren't even needed. Derek could feel Shawndra's pulse racing through her body. The heat of the moment made his blood rush downward, tempting him to think with his manhood instead of his brain.

Using the same hand that was just on her ass a second ago, he slid it around the curve of her hip, down her thigh, and parked it in the warm aperture of her pussy. He could hear the soft moan slip between her clenched teeth and trembling lips.

"Derek . . . what are you doin', baby?" she asked, fighting back a grin as she tried to hold her composure. "You know we can't do this right now. Them people should be here any minute."

The knock at the front door damn near made both of them jump out of their skin.

"Yo!! Get it Right Renovations! Is anybody home!?" a man hollered, loud enough for his voice to bounce through the whole damn house. "They gotta be in here." He poked his head through the half-open door, eyes sweeping the place like he was checking for squatters. "We have an appointment with a Derek Brown."

Three more dudes stood behind him—his crew—hard hats in hand, looking like they'd been on job sites since sunrise.

"Yeah, we right here, brah." Derek called out, glancing down at his wristwatch. "Y'all boys a little early and everything." he smirked. "y'all ain't about to start taxing already, is it?" Derek expresses with a sense of humor. "Naw, we ain't on that brah." The leader of the team clarified surely.

"I'm Just messing with y'all." Derek cracked a laugh to show he was playin', but the way his voice carried, it still had a little boss in it. "Y'all good to come in. we couldn't wait for y'all to get here honestly." The renovation crew Entered the house and slowly begins to set up their tools.

Shawndra stood there, arms folded, half-smiling, staring at the men. Always the one to be on point she eyed the team feeling out their energy's. The other half of her expression looked as if she was watching a handful of fools, clowning around, in a packed car.

"Naw, you straight, bossman," the foreman said, speaking for his squad. "Shit, we joke all damn day on site. Believe me, we be trying to get it in and get out," he admitted with a light chuckle. "Trust me, I don't think you want to open that door anyway. Cause when these fools get to joking around, I have a hard time putting them in chill mode." Following the comment, the crew of men shared looks between one another letting out a few chuckles. It wasn't long before they started laughing for real, slapping each other's shoulders and shit.

"Long as the job get done right, I ain't trippin'. By all means, enjoy yourselves," Derek confirmed. "I mean," One of the crew members said out loud to himself while cutting a side eye around the room, "we are Get it Right Renovations." The man's boss lightly sucked his teeth trying not to curse the man out for his sarcastic remark. Thankfully, the statement did no harm. Instead, it gave the room something else to laugh at. "Right, good point." Derek had to agree. "That's 'ight though, dead ass. It's nothin' better than lovin' the job you do. Besides, I took the time to read over your company's reviews, and the comments were remarkable. Plus, that four-point-eight-star rating didn't hurt my opinion either. Not to mention, I love the fact you're a Richmond-based company. I'ma always try to support the home team first—if they worth the support."

"Ain't that the truth," one of the crew members said, standin' right beside his boss.

"We appreciate the support," the head of the crew spoke up. "And we can assure you everything gon' be done to the best of our ability. As a matter of fact, we pulled up a few minutes early so we could get the time we need to set up whatever equipment we might need, check around, and get a quick mental picture of how we wanna start. And of course," he grinned, "we gone need them extra few minutes to joke and bullshit around." He smirked. "Other than that, I promise you the very best service we can give. For real, by the time we're done with this house, you might wanna throw some extra cash, just for the hell of it. We go above and beyond every time. It ain't nevers failed."

"Yeah, boss—except that one old lady," one of the crew members cut in, laughin' under his breath. "Seemed like every time we did more than what was expected, she'd have another complaint 'bout how she wanted shit different, or how she thought we shoulda did somethin' a certain way."

"You right," the bossman agreed without hesitation. "And she was the same woman who sold that same house for two hundred fifty thousand dollars—after puttin' about a hundred thousand worth of renovations into it. That raised the value up to almost six hundred thousand."

The whole room got quiet, everybody thinkin' about them numbers. Before anybody could finish doin' the math in their heads, the head man threw out another one.

"The person that bought that same house for two-fifty turned right back 'round and sold it for a whopping seven hundred fifty thousand dollars!"

Every time he told that story, it still amazed him how shit could flip— not just in the real estate game, but in life, period.

"Guess it don't pay to think you know it all, huh?" one of the crewmen said, soundin' more like a statement than a question.

"Hell naw, it don't," the boss replied, before keepin' on. "And just in case them numbers went over anybody's head, that's a hundred fifty thousand over market value—after already gettin' the house for three hundred fifty thousand less than what it was supposed to sell for. That's a half-million-dollar profit off a two-fifty investment."

"Damn, her ass should have spent some of that money and hired an agent with it."

The conversation went on as Derek and Shawndra stood by, hanging on to every word being said. Derek was super invested, which enhanced his interest as well. Shawndra, on the other hand, always paid very close attention to detail for the means of making sure everything stays in line with her man's business. She was not dumb and knew fair as well that at this point, if Derek drowned, then she was going right along with him. They were on the same boat at the end of the day. Therefore, she would do anything to guarantee that it doesn't happen.

"She was informed too. But was sure that she didn't need one. Said she knew exactly what she was doing," the boss clarified.

"Well, her loss. Guess she never heard of *make it count.* Shit, I could have advised her to do better than that."

The group shared another laugh.

"No bullshit. But you live and you learn. And as for us, it's time that we get to work and handle this business at hand. Let's get to it."

The men started to gather up their equipment and tools and headed to their stations.

"If there's anything we can help you with, please feel more than welcome to let us know. I am a very hands-on person," Derek had his hand extended, awaiting a handshake from the boss of the company. "And thank you again for taking on the job."

"No problem, Mr. Brown. It's our duty. Thanks for choosing *Get It Right Renovations.* But no, we got it from here. However, if there are any last-minute changes that you would like to add in, please try to get the request a few days before our expected finishing date arrives, so we could have the proper time to set everything in place."

"Will do. Although, I'm pretty sure that we have our minds made up. If any changes should be made, then it came from the fiancée," Derek joked, tapping the shoulder of the company's boss, cutting his eye over at Shawndra.

"Don't do me like that, Boo. I'm the one that picked most of the designs out," she made clear.

"Like I said, if things change, you know where they came from."

The two men laughed harmlessly at the manly inside joke.

"Trust me, I've been doing this for a long time now. I don't think there's anything I haven't seen thus far. You two take care of yourself now. You have my number, and I have yours. I'll give you a call if I have any questions or concerns. Seeing that it's a few things that need to be done in a few rooms, it shouldn't take us that long to finish up at all. I'll say three months tops. With our working effort and speed, we usually cut our timing down by almost forty percent. We'll be giving a seven-day heads-up call when we're almost finished."

"Okay, I appreciate that. And trust me, we'll be popping up every now and then to see how the process is coming along. So, don't be surprised if I walk through the door one day and catch you all bullshitting around," Derek expressed one of those harsh jokes again, making it hard to tell if he was even joking at all.

"If you can catch that happening, I'll dock our pay for you."

"Deal."

Derek and the boss man shook hands one last time before Derek headed out the door, on to his next mission.

Lesson 3.5
Pivotal Moments

Shy dropped back three, maybe four steps, spikes on the bottom of his sneakers grinding dirt as the D-line came crashing in like a stampede. Wild-Boy, posted wide to his right, shot off the line with that full-speed burst—chest out, arms pumping, cleats slicing the turf. Within seconds, he was gone, leaving the corner looking stupid and burnt.

"Put it up Lil' Brah!" Wild-Boy yelled out to his little brother holding down the quarterback spot.

Shy evaded a lineman attempting to tackle him and advanced several significant strides down the field. Next, he cocked his arm back and released it with all his passion and might while thrusting his arm back forward. Shy, the other players on the field, along with the sideline and entire bleachers, kept their eyes on the ball as it sailed high and long through the air like an eagle looking to swoop down on its prey.

The oval-shaped brown piece of leather began declining, soon to drop down on its target. Wild-Boy kicked it up another gear, giving it all he had to make sure he was where he needed to be when the ball reached its destination. As fast as the ball flew, as fast as Wild-Boy's legs kicked up turf from the field, and as fast as everyone's hearts raced in their chests, somehow everything had seemed to be going in super slow motion.

With both hands, Wild-Boy reached as far into the air as he could while keeping his eyes locked on the sight of the football. Measuring it with his natural athletic abilities, he quickly realized he would have to change plans fast if he was going to be able to get his hands on the ball. After about five more steps, the ball was connecting to his right hand that he had stretched out, anticipating the arrival of the falling ball. Wild-Boy immediately cuffed the ball into his chest while stumbling as he fought to keep his balance. Within no time, he was back in stride, picking his speed back up.

Suddenly, he was able to hear the screams from the attendees of the game. The long wait was over now, and it was a race to the end zone. Wild-Boy sprinted down the field like a cheetah hunting a gazelle.

Shy was almost certain of what would happen next. Wild-Boy and him did this repeatedly two or three times a game. With that, Shy was already making his way toward the end zone, yelling motivating phrases to hype his brother up even more.

"Go nigga! You got this! This our shit! Let's fuckin' go!"

This touchdown was a little more special. With the clock ticking down to the last few seconds of the game, this touchdown would place the Hillside Warriors in the perfect position to become the champions for the Richmond City Recreations Football League.

Right before crossing the line into the end zone, Wild-Boy leaped off his feet, jumping high into the air, flipping frontwards, sticking the landing perfectly on his two feet like a gymnast. The rest of the team was there immediately, sweeping Wild-Boy off his feet and holding him high up in the air as if he was the trophy himself.

Wild-Boy spotted Shy approaching and pointed him out. "Get his ass!" he yelled out to his teammates. On demand, another group of Hillside Warriors were throwing Shy in the air, bouncing him and bopping as they yelled, screamed, and celebrated.

Once all the hype calmed down and the celebrations were coming to an end, Keem pulled up on his two younger brothers with a message.

"Y'all niggas come on, brah!" he yelled out, catching the attention of the two. "Ma and Dad waitin' on y'all. Dad said y'all can bring whoever y'all wanna bring. But he also said everybody must bring they asses on now, or else they gone get left!"

The two football stars grabbed up a handful of their favorite teammates each, then they all quickly followed behind Keem.

Waiting for them in the parking lot were their parents along with a handful of other adults.

"You two were so amazing out there. I am very proud of you both. Y'all had another wonderful season, and this year, all the hard work paid off with a championship," their mother expressed, her glee showing for her two youngest children.

"That's right!" their father added in, even more excited than his wife. "We got us a young Peyton Manning and Marvin Harrison. Y'all deserve to pick where we eatin' from tonight. Wherever y'all wanna go, it's all on us."

After the brothers argued and debated about where they would eat at, the entourage loaded the vehicles and headed off to their destination.

"Brah, I swear to God, if you would have threw that ball the wrong way, I would still be beatin' the shit out you right now as we speak," Wild-Boy said right before stuffing his mouth with a slice of pizza.

"Nigga, you know I don't never throw the ball wrong," a younger version of Shy replied, fully confident.

"Yeah whatever! That pick you threw right after the openin' of the fourth quarter almost cost us the game," Keem reminded, deadeye locked on Shy.

"But you shook back though, and that's all that matters," their father added in.

After the buffet, Shy's father and his team of hustlers, who helped sponsor the team, took the young football stars to indulge in a few games of laser tag, paintball shootin', an all-around arcade, and go-kart racing.

Keem was way ahead of the bunch in the race. At this moment, Wild-Boy and Shy competed for second place. It wasn't anything new — the two were always very competitive at any and everything they could compete in.

Wild-Boy swerved recklessly, trying to run Shy clean off the course. Shy, knowing the antics of his brother's behavior, expected the attempt, slowed down just enough, turned the wheel hard to the left, waited for Wild-Boy's go-kart to cross over in front of his, then slammed his foot on the gas pedal until it was smashed down on the floor.

Shy's go-kart sped right past Wild-Boy's. As it did, he laughed loud and hard while sticking up his middle finger toward Wild-Boy, who was now a few carts behind him.

To say that Wild-Boy was pissed off would be an understatement. He was so furious that it didn't take long for him to end up right back on Shy's tail. The other drivers were so afraid to cross Wild-Boy's path that they deliberately drove clean out his way.

About a half a lap, a few turns, and a speeding thirty seconds later, Shy could barely believe that Wild-Boy was damn near neck to neck with him. Before he knew it, he was right back in the same situation he was in just a few seconds ago.

As he always did, Wild-Boy had underestimated his little brother. This time, he knew he'd have to be a little slicker and at least one step ahead of the next move. Wild-Boy knew that Shy thought of him as a rash individual. Therefore, he would use Shy's way of thinking to his advantage.

This time, Wild-Boy was on the right side instead of the left. With that, Wild-Boy swerved wide right, hoping that Shy would prepare for him to come back heavily left. Anticipating his expectations, Shy repeated his actions from a moment ago. To his surprise, instead of trying to slam into his go-kart, Wild-Boy was rounding the corner, officially taking the lead for the second-place position.

With Shy trying his old trick, it caused him to swerve sharply right, coming inches away from crashing into the track's border. Unfortunately, before he could, a speeding go-kart collided with his. He tried his best to gain control—safe to say, it was a second too late.

While turning the wheel hard left, Shy ran into the border, causing his go-kart to come up off two of its wheels. A split second afterward, another go-kart crashed into him for the second time. Shy's go-kart flipped. Next, his sight—along with his hearing—went blank.

***

Shy's eyes popped wide open as he came back to the present from the coma he'd been in for the past two days. The neck brace wrapped around his head made it impossible for him to move his head left or right. He knew from the lights embedded in the ceiling, the railings he felt on the bed, the smell of the room, the tubes in his nose, and the IV in his arm exactly where he was.

"Hey, baby! I've been waiting days for you to wake up. Glad I didn't miss it. I swear I was about to go and get me something to eat."

Shy also knew exactly whose voice it was that he was hearing. She leaned over and pressed her soft lips against his crusty and ashy ones.

"Your lips dry as a bitch." Her expression was out of concern. "I'ma bring you back somethin' to drink with your food. But for now, you can drink this ice water I made for you not too long ago. It's better for you anyway."

She grabbed the oversized peach hospital cup, pressed a button adjusting the leverage of the bed, and held the straw close to his lips so he could sip from the cup.

"What the fuck happened?" Shy asked Destiny after gulping down multiple sips of water from the straw.

"I'm sure I don't have the whole story. All I know is that I received a call from my cousin that you were in a terrible car accident."

As Destiny spoke, flashes of the last thing Shy could remember started to run across his brain. He thought about the shootout. A mental motion picture of the man's head busting open, with blood splashing out like a cherry-flavored Gusher, replayed in his head.

The image reminded him that he was the shooter who caused the bullet to slam into that man's head. I fuckin' killed somebody, he thought to himself, causing the exact emotions from that night to come rushing back through his body.

Damn.

Thinking deeper into the situation, Shy began to give less fucks once he realized the reason for his actions. A nigga tried to kill my fuckin' brother. Shit, I'll do it all over again if I have to.

Destiny was still yappin' on. To Shy's ears, it was only muffled mumbles. His next thought was the car chase that led to the accident.

After some time, Shy wanted to know, "Where's my brother?" He turned to ask Destiny as if he was certain she had ever met Keem a day in her life.

"Shy, I don't even know who your brother is," she admitted. "But a handful of men lookin' like they were a few years older than us did come up here to check on you. They had some woman with 'em too. They didn't say much to me but left a message for you. Somethin' about makin' it count or somethin'."

As Destiny talked, it hit Shy like a ton of bricks that Destiny was standing there by his bedside. Even though he didn't have many people to choose from, not in a hundred years would he have expected Destiny to be the one here waiting for him to heal.

"Come on! We have to get out of here."

His mind was already racing. So, on impulse, Shy attempted to leap out of the bed.

"Aaaaah!" he screamed out once, feeling the pain in his legs for the first time.

"Your legs are not healed yet, babe. Your doctor says that it may take a few days, and he suggests that you fully take part in the physical therapy that he has provided for you."

Shy took a quick second to think about what Destiny had just revealed to him.

"Fuck!" he forced through clenched teeth. It took everything in him not to scream it out, but the extra frustration was written all over his face.

Destiny laid a soft hand lightly on Shy's chest. Before laying him back down, she rubbed and caressed the body where his heavy heart rested.

"I know you are very anxious right now, Shy. But I'm not going to allow you to go anywhere—at least not so soon. You need to take your time and heal properly. Especially if you plan to do something stupid once you get out of here."

You would've thought Destiny had the power of persuasion the way she was able to calm Shy's temperament so quickly.

"Are you okay?" she asked him for clarification.

He nodded to say, yes.

"Good. Now I'm gonna head downstairs and grab something to eat for us before everything tries to close on us. You got anything in mind that you'd like to try?"

"It don't matter for real, Boo. I'm good with whatever you get."

Shy rubbed his hand over his fuzzy dreads while slumping back down into the bed, trying to get as comfortable as he could in this time of uncertainty.

"If you can, just make sure you grab me an orange juice. And let the nurse know I need to holla at her. My fuckin' head is killin' me right now."

"Whatever you need, Boo, I got you."

Destiny was making her way toward the door at the time she assured Shy that she'd cover his request. As she did, Shy thought it would be best to close his eyes and rest his brain. This might be the only time he'd have to allow everything to process through his thoughts. Even though it was a lot, it'd be the only way he could move forward.

Heading to the elevator, Destiny pulled her phone out, opening her music app. Next, she searched for her AirPods so she could use her Bluetooth. Before she could realize that the case was missing, she was being bumped over aggressively by a man she had never seen a day in her life.

He was moving fast. So, after her slight stumbling, she turned her head expeditiously, looking to get a mental picture of the rude individual.

"Damn! Excuse you," Destiny uttered just loud enough for the man to hear.

"Fuck you, bitch!" she thought she heard him say. Although, the movement of his lips was the confirmation she needed to know she wasn't hearing things.

The first person she thought about was Shy. She knew if he was there, he'd protect her without question. Then, she set her thoughts back on what her mind had been focused on before that seven-second bad experience. That's when she noticed she didn't have what she was looking for.

Frustrated, Destiny released a small sigh, realizing she'd have to make her way back to the elevator—unless she decided to take the stairs instead. By the time she made her way back, she noticed the rude man stepping onto the only available elevator going up—the same direction she needed to travel.

She was thankfully a healthy young woman, so she'd rather take the stairs before sharing a small space with that asshole. With the motion of a light jog, Destiny made it to her destined floor right as the elevator dinged.

She found it extremely irritating to see the same man she'd been avoiding now stepping off the elevator on the same floor.

Only to buy herself some time and separation, Destiny took a detour to the ladies' room. She stared into the mirror, forcing herself to regain control over her mind. Honestly, it made no sense to her why this stranger was bothering her so much. Other than the bump—which she was starting to convince herself was done purposefully—what other reason did she have to feel this worried about an unknown man?

He should be wherever he was on his way to by now, Destiny told herself mentally, right before stepping out of the restroom.

As expected, her sights were clear of the man. She approached the desk and showed her visitor's pass dangling from her shirt.

"Baby, you know I know who you are. How's your friend doing?" the receptionist at the desk asked Destiny.

Within the last few days of seeing each other so much, they'd had plenty of small talk, learning enough about each other through those exchanges.

"Crazy you asked," Destiny responded, standing in front of the double doors waiting for them to open. "Because he just got up a few minutes before I left the room. I'm tryin' to go get him somethin' to eat right now. I just forgot something."

By the time Destiny finished her sentence, the doors were opening, and she was rushing through them.

"That's good to hear!" the receptionist had to shout out due to the speeding pace of Destiny's walk. "Tell him I hope he has a speedy recovery!"

Less than a minute later, Destiny was approaching the doors to Shy's room. Not wanting to startle him in case he was resting, she eased through the door, trying not to make too much noise as she entered.

Once again, Destiny thought her mind was playing tricks on her. As she focused on her hearing a little more, she could hear a struggle coming from Shy's hospital bed. At first, she thought he was having health complications.

That was until her eyesight matched the sounds in her ears.

She could hardly believe it. Yet deep down inside, she had a silent knowing. It was the same rude man who had bumped her downstairs not too long ago.

He had both hands clamped over Shy's nose and mouth, trying to suffocate him down to his very last breath.

Doing the first thing that came to mind, Destiny screamed, "Help!" toward the hallway, hoping someone would hear her cry.

"Help! Please, somebody help me!" She was forced to scream out a couple more times. "He's trying to kill him!"

The suddenly alarmed intruder reacted by escaping from Shy's bedside and rushing out the room's door. Not really thinking before she reacted, Destiny stuck a foot out, using it to trip the man up.

He stumbled, nearly falling to the floor. Catching himself with both hands, he was soon back on his feet and off running again.

"It's him!" Destiny screamed again, this time directing her words to a group of nurses and VCU policemen now running down the hallway from the other end.

The nurses rushed into the room to check on Shy, while the officers continued to pursue the suspect before he could make a clean escape.

"Please, get him before he gets away!"

Really, there was nowhere for him to go. The double doors at the hallway's end were locked. The only way they would open was with a keycard or a push of a button behind the nurse's desk sitting in the middle of the hallway.

Even if he took the time to go back for the button, it'd still be too late. Seeing this caused the man to slow down some, considering where he could run to next. Even worse, the officers were on his tail.

"Freeze! Right now!" the lead officer on the scene yelled toward the man, his already drawn pistol held high. "Do not make this worse than what it already is!"

The man stopped dead in his tracks, taking the handful of seconds he had to contemplate his next move. Before he could even imagine planning an escape that was nowhere in sight, he was receiving orders from the law.

"Do not take one more step. Put your hands up behind your head and slowly make your way to the ground. Please, no sudden moves. I want to help you get through this situation as smooth as I can."

Knowing his fate, the man took a deep sigh right before following the policeman's demands.

"Go in, now!" the lead officer barked, sending orders to one of his fellow officers. "Apprehend him—but take it easy. I gave my word, and he complied."

The officer taking orders placed the cuffs on the man while reading him his Miranda Rights.

"You have the right to remain silent . . . Anything you say can and will be used . . ."

The lead officer of the VCU Police walked over to the spot of the arrest and waited while the suspect was being brought to his feet.

"Exactly what were you doing in there?" the officer asked. He was more curious than anything else—almost forgetting this would now be an active open investigation.

The man looked the officer dead in his eyes and sucked his teeth, like he had a piece of steak stuck between them and was trying to get it out.

"I have my rights, right?" he asked—honest but sarcastic.

"Yes, sir, you do. Get him out of here. Guess we'll see you in court."

Once the nurses gave him some oxygen, checked his vitals, and made sure he was okay, Destiny was back by Shy's bedside.

"Are you okay?" she wanted to know.

"Yeah, I'm good. Just mad as a bitch," Shy replied, trying to hold his anger with everything he had in him.

"Do you know who that man was?" Destiny continued, feeding her curiosity.

"Hell naw. I don't think I ever seen that nigga a day in my life, for real," Shy assured her.

"That's weird," she confirmed.

"As a bitch." That was Shy's only reply.

Lesson 3.6
Don't Cry Over Spilled Milk

"Motherfucker!" Keem released a frustrating scream as he tossed his phone with as much strength that he could muster. The iPhone flew across the room hitting the wall, falling into pieces to the floor of the condo. "I want niggas watching my fucking brother twenty-four seven as long as he in that mother fucking hospital. And Mia…"

"Yeah, boss, what you need me to do?" Mia was tentative, awaiting the command of Keem's orders.

"I need you to hit the lawyer up, like *now*. We're suing that whole fucking hospital. 'Cause for the life of me, I can't figure out how the fuck they let a nigga just walk straight to the back like that. No security, no nothing. Fuck—when my baby was born, they damn near strip-searched me just to let me in the room. Somebody gon' answer for this shit. *Somebody paying* for this fuck up

"Well, big dawg, you know the jail should be done processing him in within the next hour or two. That way we can check the records or whatever else we need to and at least get a name of who the nigga is," Simon advised — one of the first and best plans Keem had heard from his lieutenants since his understandable outburst.

"That's a good point, Simon," Keem admitted. "If I wasn't so fucking pissed off, I would have thought of that simple ass shit myself. But I'm glad you were able to do what you are supposed to do. Which is to pick a nigga up when I'm down like this."

After his statement, Keem took a seat. He figured he needed to think this whole thing through — or at least calm down enough to hear the rest of his team out, just in case they did come up with some good ideas.

"Yeah, and on top of that," Blick was adding on to his right-hand man's assumptions, "by the time we had got there after getting the call from that chick Shy's been talking to, we found this." He held up a 5th Ward chain, hanging from his clamped fist. It was one of the exact same chains Keem had snatched from the nigga's neck — the nigga that had died in the car crash. With the dummy dead, Keem knew these 5th Ward niggas were trying hard to assassinate any and every member of his OGS squad. Not only had they come for him, but without even giving a chance in hell to retaliate, they'd fucked up even more by trying his brother.

"Why the fuck is these broke-ass 5th Ward niggas at our necks like—" Switch started, but Keem shut him out. Not because he wasn't trying to hear him, but because he already knew where Switch was going with the question. The truth was, only Keem knew the real answer to what Switch was getting at. Keem had yet to tell his team — or anyone else — what happened in Petersburg. He felt like he couldn't, because if he did it might raise suspicions of why. For the life of him he could not expose himself to killing P and his sister Roxy, or even explain why, for that matter.

"This what I think we should do—" Blick began, but Keem had focused his hearing back on the room and cut him off.

"Naw," Keem finally spoke up after sitting silent and stuck in his thoughts for some time. "This what we are going to do. We're going to keep up with his court-date timing and process, like Simon suggested. That way we can know everything that's going. One of y'all go and tell Mia while she's on the phone now to have her pull his booking photo and badge his name—make sure we got the right fool. Tell her to post a runner at the courthouse the day he bonds so we know exactly who walks out. And as soon as he does, we snatch his ass up and figure out exactly what the fuck is going on and see what these 5th Ward niggas are trying to get out this crash-dummy mission-ass shit."

"Already, say no more, Keem. We on top of all of that," Simon assured the leader. "Until then, you good on everything else? You need one of us to roll up some gas or something?"

"Naw, I'm good, Si. Good lookin'." Keem responded. "Just bring me a bottle and a cup. And make sure everyone clears the room for me. I need some time to think, clear my head and shit like that. Thank you, appreciate it."

"Alright, y'all heard the man," Simon called out as he made his way to the minibar. "Let's clear the room. Everybody needs to get back to their jobs. If you're post-control, make sure them niggas ain't out there slacking. If you were runnin' errands, go pick that bread up and make sure it's all there before you bring it back. Come on, y'all niggas know what to do — I shouldn't have to run it down. Ayee, Switch, make sure them niggas in line."

By the end of his sentence most of the room had already cleared out, the last handful of bodies exiting through the door. Simon chose Keem's favorite brand of liquor, grabbed the favorite glass he loved to sip out of, and carried it over to the chair where Keem reclined.

"Here you go, my nigga," he said, placing the bottle and glass on the table.

"I know we've faced a lot of shit together. And even though shit never really hit as close to home as this, we always come out on top. This shit is no different. You a smart-ass nigga, with a strong and loyal-ass team. I have the utmost faith that you'll find a way to see us through this storm — just like all the rest of them." Keem sat silent as a lamb, listening to the encouraging words of his long-term friend and now business partner.

"So, take all the time you need to think this shit through and come up with the best solution for yourself and the team. We will prevail. You don't have to worry or stress about nothing that's goin' on out here. I'm gonna be on top of these motherfuckers like cream of chicken poured over turkey wings. You just focus on what's on your mind. Do some meditating or some shit like that," Simon chuckled. "But seriously, maybe something will come to you out the blue."

Keem began pouring his troubles into the glass. "Once again," he said before taking a sip, "I appreciate you. I really do. For everything. It was because of you that a lot of this shit was even possible. I hear you though — loud and clear. You can go and make sure niggas continue to handle the business. I got this part here. Thank you for the prep talk and advice, coach. Now get the fuck out!"

Simon chuckled as he left the room. "If I'm the coach, you must be the owner then, boss. Catch you later though, and you already know to call me if you need me." He headed down the hallway.

The smile on his face slowly faded as the seriousness of the situation came to mind. He could sense the tenseness of Keem's anxiety. Keem had always kept his cool through any situation no matter how difficult, but with the latest events piling up one by one, they'd been peeling layers off Keem's confidence — dulling the sharpness of his wits and assurance. To Simon it was like Keem was beginning to doubt himself, which was something he'd never seen in all his life. It was as if Keem was suddenly hit with regret, reasoning with himself instead of being that man of procrastination. Simon couldn't put a finger on exactly why Keem was shifting; other than that the person he'd worked so hard to protect was now one of the main targets of a newfound enemy. Whatever it was, the only thing Simon knew for certain was Keem would have to snap back into shape fast. Because if he didn't, the captain could lose control of the boat, causing it to lose its way, or worse, sink. And Simon would be damned if he stood by and watched that happen.

Lesson 3.7
What's Meant Will Be

"Alright Foster, it's your time to shine. Make it count." A female correction officer gave him a quick nod, voice tough but halfway soft, like she low-key wanted to see him make it. "I don't wanna see your ass back in here."

E ain't nothing. Just stared straight ahead, jaws tight, eyes cold. The CO slid her key card, and the door gave that long, ugly buzz. One more heavy-ass metal door, one more step— then boom—that outside air hit him. First taste of freedom in damn near forever. She ain't know though. E wasn't walking out lost or scared. He was charged up. Heart beating steady. He had his shit lined up stacked from the inside, a plan locked tight, and his rider still holding him down. The same one who never folded when he was at the bottom. The one who was able and willing to make it all happen with him. The same person that he was now walking out of the last door of the jail and looking for. Granted, she was an employee of the same jail that he was incarcerated. But for some reason, E still expected her to be right there when he walked out of those doors. Besides, it was something that they had discussed multiple times.

Now that the time was here and she wasn't, it made him feel like a fool. It didn't mean much to him that most of his ex-felons were watching from the windows, banging on them to show their celebration for his freedom. E knew the routine and heard the sounds, but he halfway ignored them, keeping his eyes focused on the parking lot scanning for the description of Crawford's vehicle.

Without looking back, he threw up the gang sign with two of his fingers and thumb sticking out. Once he did, the sounds got so loud he could even hear their voices yelling and screaming through the thick-ass glass. E kept pushing through the parking lot. Already, he figured his plans would have to be reconsidered. Seeing that the very first step to his plan wasn't in its proper place pissed him off. As usual, E did his best to keep a cool, humble demeanor. But on the inside, he was burning up—hotter than Juvenile's wildest track.

E replayed the first conversation he ever had with Tiara Crawford in his mind—the one about the brand-new vehicle she had copped with some of the money they'd run up together. A 2024 Kia EV9 GT-Line. E almost had a fit when he asked what the total price of the fast electric-charging car was and she said, "Seventy-seven thousand, six hundred twenty-six dollars." That was until she assured him she'd only put ten grand down, with a credit score of seven hundred fifty-three. That cooled him off quick and even got him hype. After that, they were back vibin', talking about the ride's features and what they planned to do with it once he came home.

Now though, it was clear the bitch had straight played him like a sucker. The only reason he halfway denied it in his mind was because he'd used her too in the beginning. The pain hit different because he caught feelings for her. He not only believed her; he trusted her. This moment was starting to feel too much like what BM had done to him before. Which brought his focus back to one of the main aims of his mission.

"Fuck that bitch," he mumbled under his breath. After all, he'd damn near made two hundred bands with the woman.

E was almost out the parking lot when he hit a pause at the bus stop sitting on the sidewalk. He looked up and down the street one more time, making sure he hadn't overlooked the car he was searching for. The streets were dead. Only two cars sat still at the red light. Taking a deep breath, E started walking up the hill toward Mosby Court Projects—another default in his plans.

He knew damn well it was a bad idea to pop back up on the block fresh out. Especially since nobody even knew he was a free man yet. With the plans he had for BM, showing his face would fuck everything up—put him at a disadvantage, especially being naked out here with no tool to protect himself.

With nowhere else to go, what else could he do? His mind started racing, trying to come up with the quickest plan to avoid the worst. Different scenarios spun through his head so fast he almost missed the vehicle creeping up beside him—quiet like a stalking tiger.

Coming to his senses, E finally looked right and laid eyes on a 2024 Mercedes-Benz GLC 300 AWD 4MATIC. The windows were too tinted to see through. For a minute, E almost panicked. He thought about taking off through the shortcut woods that led into Mosby. The only person really on his mind was BM. Even though E was almost sure BM ain't know about his release, he knew better than to put anything past him.

His thoughts were sliding deep into paranoia until the passenger-side window rolled down just enough for him to see who the driver was.

To his expected surprise, it was Tiara Crawford. Last time E checked, she was pushing a Kia—he guessed she upgraded while he was gone.

E's heart skipped a beat like he was face-to-face with his biggest opponent. Although, the skipping of his heart wasn't for that reason. It was reasoned to being cared for. It was the point of him being dead ass wrong about her loyalty. It was like the vision of his biggest dreams unfolding right in front of his eyes.

"Hey, Boo," Tiara shouted through the window from behind the wheel. She placed the gear in park, jumped out, and hurriedly ran around the car meeting E at the front of it. Tightly they hugged before they passionately shared a kiss.

"Hurry up and get your ass in the car so we can go. You, driving." The actions of her moves matched her words as she jumped into the passenger seat as fast as she could.

"You thought I ghosted your ass, didn't you?" she asked the obvious simultaneously as E was pulling the car away from the curb.

E smirked from embarrassment and shook his head. Not to say no though, but as in, *I can't believe she really pulled up and came through.*

"Yeah, you did," she managed to say through her chuckles. "I know you, Boo. That's fucked up though that you thought I'd do you like that. You must don't believe me when I tell you that I love your ugly ass. But you had to know I couldn't have just picked you up right in front of the jail. I mean, I know you're free now and all, but if we plan to go through with our moves then we don't need to raise not one bit of suspicion. You feel me?"

"Yeah, I feel you, Babe. Shit does make sense. And I'm glad you're thinking ahead of the game. That's how we gone beat the competition at everything we do," E agreed. "But why the hell you ain't tell me about this car though? I see you got the thirty-day tags on this bitch and everything. How long you had it?"

"Oh yeah," Tiara vocalized as if she had honestly forgotten about something. "Surpriisseee! I got a car for you, Boo. I hope you really like it!" Tiara was all out excited, as if someone had just bought her a brand-new car instead of it being the other way around.

"Oh, this my shit?" E asked, shocked. "How much did this joint cost?"

Tiara sucked her teeth lightly, rolling her eyes but clearly unfazed. "You always wanna know the price of something, like we some broke motherfuckers or something, Babe. We are having shit out here. Motion, our way, it's giving 'ain't tricking if you got it' type shit."

E laughed. She was right, so he agreed by repeating, "type shit."

"Anyway," E decided to change the subject. "Where the hell we about to go?" he asked.

"Shidd, wherever you wanna go, Babe. The world is yours!" Tiara replied confidently. "Naw, but for real," she said, reaching for the screen sitting in the middle of the dashboard. "We gone head to the crib right quick. Get you cleaned up, fed with some real food, get that dick wet, get fly as fuck, chill for a few hours or so. I swear I dreamt every night of just lying up in bed under your arms, wrapped up in your warm body while you held me tightly until I fell fast asleep. Bitch ain't gotta dream no more. My motherfucking man is home, bitch!"

The excitement was clear through her speech. "Then once we do get up, we can head out and continue this mission we on. I got you most of the clothes you wanted already, so you gone be without a doubt stepping out dripping on these niggas out here. I did save you some room in your closet because I figured you may want to do some shopping on your own. Are you cool with the plans and all that, or do you have something else in mind?"

"Naw, all that's gravy," E assured. "Ain't a need to rush at all. Plus, to be honest, you are the only thing I have in mind right now. You over there looking sexy as hell."

The compliment sent Tiara into a wave of lovely feelings. "I know right!" The smile on her face was as wide as the Atlantic Ocean. "Thank you, Boo. I dead ass wanted to make sure I look my best for your first time seeing me in real clothes. Oh, but don't trip though, this your bitch every day. Even on my worst day I'm looking way better than most bitches."

E was humored by her confidence. It turned him on even more than he already was. "Trust me, I ain't tripping. And

43

I'm not worried about what these other bitches got going. Shidd, you bad as a motherfucker. But on top of all that, your ass the realest, dead ass."

Tiara looked over at E and admired his features deeply. It was the first time she was able to stare at him without any interruptions. It seemed as if he became even more handsome every second she looked at him. With her left hand, she reached over and placed it in E's lap.

"Every real nigga needs a real bitch." Her statement was followed by her soft hand caressing E's right thigh. "Damn, I can't wait to get your sexy ass home," her words came out through her clenched teeth in a half moan.

She stretched her hand out further until it was placed on the area of his dick. Gripping it with passion, she gave it a light massage through his jeans. Next, she used her other hand to aid her for what she was about to do next, which was to unbutton and unzip his pants.

She pulled his tool out of the toolbox, leaned over, and gave it a big kiss. E's little man at once grew up standing as tall as the Statue of Liberty. E remained silent, trying his best to stay focused on the road. It was very tempting for him not to lay his head on the headrest and shut his eyes.

After a couple more kisses added with a few more licks, she finally and smoothly eased the dick into her mouth. At first, she sucked with a calm pace and motion, but before long, she was mopping the dick up like she had a gun to her head. Slurping and sucking up all the juices that tried to go too far.

E enjoyed the ride. Even though it had only been about ten or fifteen minutes, so far everything had been going great. And he couldn't imagine a better way of coming home than this. One thing he did imagine though was just how much better it was about to get. What more could a nigga with a past like his ask for? His time had finally come.

Lesson 3.8
Regardless, Keep Grinding

After merging onto I-395 North not too long ago, Pickle took the Exit 4 ramp toward Maine Avenue/SW Waterfront/National Park. Beside him in the passenger seat was BM. The back seats were taken up by Shoota and Bank. They were heading to a meet-up location in Southwest Washington, D.C.

"Why every time we come up here these niggas gotta switch up the location?" Pickle wanted to know for a good reason. This was only their third trip to D.C., and even though each one had gotten a little less confusing than the first, it was the changing directions of the meet-up spot that kept the driver from getting too familiar with the route.

Pickle was always the one who had to drive whenever an out-of-town trip was involved, because he was the only one who had sense enough to go out and obtain his driver's license. For most of the gang, it was a roadblock in their path because of all the criminal charges they had caught so far. Of course, it wasn't impossible—but at their age, considering that they could do whatever they wanted to, including driving, the thought of owning a driver's license was barely on their mind. And that's where Pickle came into play. He had one thing to offer that no one else could, and it finally came in handy for situations like this.

"They think that by switching up the address they keeping us from getting used to their city's streets. But what they don't know is they really helping us," BM said, handing the game down to his younger peers. "Cause instead of running to the same old spot, we get to move around. And all it take is for a nigga to pay attention to link the streets up."

"If y'all ain't noticed by now, the niggas never invited us to their home turf." By that, he meant the hood they controlled, hustled, and thugged in. "That could mean one or two things. They smart as hell not to trust OT niggas they barely know and don't want us to know their lo, thinking we gone make a move on them or something—or they just pussy as a bitch for the same exact reasons. But for real, neither one of them matters to me. I'm just here to get this money, get this hot-ass shit up out this car, and get the fuck back home."

Hidden in the trunk of the car was a whole brick of cocaine. BM, along with his YNT crew, was beginning to branch out with their business. One of BM's sharpest moves was to go outside the hood, make the money, and bring as much back home as possible. As a result, he had become a small connection for a few niggas he'd met through his networking. One person was out of Winston-Salem, North Carolina; another was in Farmville, Virginia; and the last one—the one flipping the most work—was here in Washington, D.C.

"Yeah, you right, BM," Pickle agreed, feeling no need to protest.

"Maybe we need to start making these niggas come to us," Shoota suggested.

"Yeah, that might be a good idea," Bank jumped in before BM could respond. "But then if we show them where we at, we the ones putting our shit at risk."

"Shidd, nigga, a chance on what?" Shoota asked. "I wish a nigga would pull up in my city thinking they gone take something from me or anyone else I'm eating with, for that matter."

BM stayed quiet. He figured it was better to keep his ears open, and mouth closed. It intrigued him to hear how his young bulls thought and what they had to say.

"If you wanna keep it a band," Shoota continued, "we taking a chance right now just by driving all the way this far with that shit in the trunk."

For a few long seconds, all was quiet besides the low music playing in the background.

"Naw, dead ass though," Pickle agreed with Shoota's last words.

"I can't speak for the rest," BM finally said, "but one thing about us—we ain't ever make too many moves before crossing our T's and dotting our I's. Niggas done came too far now to be out here moving like some chickens with our heads cut off."

His soldiers were all ears.

"The more we move, the farther we go. The farther we go, the smarter we get. Niggas wasn't fucking with us out the gate, but the more we learn about this game we in, through the shit we experience firsthand, eventually we gone be unstoppable. I'm talking about from every angle a nigga can think about. So if a nigga gotta put a few hundred miles on the car every now and then, so be it. We gone do this shit the smartest way—get in, get out, and get the fuck away. The only way a nigga can slip is by not listening, getting big-headed, thinking he know too fucking much, or getting on some pussy-ass shit, letting his nervous system fuck up his train of thought."

"I don't give a fuck where we gotta be or where we gotta go. If the money there, I'm there. Niggas either riding or getting the fuck out my way, dead ass."

BM's short speech shut the conversation down. There was no more to be said. Even if the boys did have an opinion, they kept it to themselves for sure.

"You sure this where these niggas told us to meet them at?" Pickle asked.

"This 1000 Maine Street, right?" BM countered.

"Yeah, but it's a parking garage," Pickle said.

"Well, get your ass up in that bitch and park then."

As soon as they rolled inside the garage, BM's eyes darted up towards the corners. Cameras were everywhere. He clocked at least four just on the first level. "Keep yo' hoodie up, nigga," he told Shoota low. "Ain't no tellin who watchin' this bitch." Pickle eased the car into a space far from the elevator and exits, tucked between two concrete columns. "Park where it's dark," BM added, still scanning. "We ain't tryin' to end up on nobody footage when shit go left."

Pickle did as he was told and pulled up to the gate of the parking garage.

"They asking for money," he said.

"Nigga, yo' ass ain't broke," BM snapped back. "Give them people that funky-ass two dollars."

Bank and Shoota let out loud spurts of laughter listening to the back-and-forth.

"You know that nigga tight pocketed as a motherfucker," Bank joked.

Once all the simple confusion was over with, the car headed to the first deck level and waited. Moments later, a car pulled up right beside them in an empty parking space. Feeding BM's happiness, it was exactly the few niggas he was waiting on.

"All our money in this bag, right?" he questioned from habit.

"Come on, man. Have we ever had a reason to short you yet?" His business opponent asked a legitimate question.

"Naw, not at all. But I ain't green either. I know how this game goes sometimes, my nigga."

All eight men present were well alert and standing on all ten of their toes.

"Man let's just get this shit done and over with so we can get the fuck up outta here. You know the drill."

The two teams went through their usual process. BM kept one eye on his crew and the other on the niggas they were dealing with, making sure no funny moves got made. Cameras might've been in the garage, but nobody was about to get caught lacking on his watch. Before you knew it, BM and YNT were back on the road, heading to Richmond, Virginia, wasting no time at all.

On the way back into their hometown, BM, Bank, and Shoota used that time to count the money up with one goal in mind—to make sure every dollar was there before they touched down on their home field.

The money-counting mission was done and over, with about twenty-five minutes left to spare on the ride. The rest of that time for BM, Pickle, and Shoota was used to rest their eyes before it was time to get back to work, while Bank took the wheel since they were so close to the city and the car was clean.

"What's up, y'all niggas got that bread, right?" That was Tru. He was the one to open the door and the first to run his mouth—irritating BM as he always did.

"Fuck you think, nigga?" BM almost felt assaulted, until he reminded himself exactly who was talking.

"Everybody at the table! It's time to get paid, and we're about to have a meeting. I got a few words for some of y'all niggas," BM announced. "Whoever ain't here already, one of y'all or somebody call them niggas up and put them on game. And do it ASAP—we got other shit to do out this motherfucker. That money ain't gone wait on no bullshitting-ass motherfucker. That's law."

Lesson 3.9
Prepare For the Worse

Keem pulled up to a secluded area surrounded mostly by woods.

"This looks like that back of the graveyard off Laburnum Avenue." Mia said what was now obvious to both her and Keem.

It was already over half an hour past midnight, so the darkness was in full control at this point.

"What the fuck this nigga got me walking into?" Keem spoke his question aloud, though he was really directing it to himself.

"Dead ass though. You want me to step out there with you?" Mia's question was full of concern. She sat in the driver's seat calmly and collectively while her eyes wandered back and forth around her surroundings.

For certain situations, Keem brings her along instead of his regular driver and number one hit man, Simon and Blick. At times, it was because their business was needed more elsewhere—or just simply because Keem felt that the situation may not be that serious.

Being that it had more to do with business, and that it was something that Mia would be able to handle with help, he felt that she was the one more accustomed to this ride along. Even though, she was just as good at shooting a firearm weapon as she was at counting them bands.

At this moment, Keem was beginning to second guess his decision to drag her along—something he's been doing a lot lately. At least when it comes to him second guessing.

"Naw, I need you to stay right here. Keep the car running just in case I need to rush back to the car and get the fuck out of here. You feel me?" Keem was already making his way out of the car while giving the instructions to Mia.

"Yeah, I feel you, my nigga. Just be smart. And please don't have a bitch out here for too long. This some creepy ass weird shit."

Keem laughed at her comment before replying, "You know I got you. I know my nigga ain't scared though?" he asked right before walking off.

"Nigga scared of what, for what?" Mia placed the already loaded pistol in her lap to emphasize exactly how unfazed she was.

"I'm just saying, if I have to come out there to get you, somebody getting laid down." She assured Keem.

"No bullshit though," Keem replied in agreement.

He walked off, making his way into the woods as he was instructed prior to his arrival. After about a good minute of walking, Keem had figured that he was already traveling too deep into the woods.

If he went any further into the woods, soon he'd be coming out on the other side entering the back of the grave. And that was something that he honestly did not want to do.

"Why the fuck would Mac link me in with this mother fucker?" he asked himself.

Stopping in his tracks, he took some time observing his surroundings. "What the fuck?"

All he was able to see was plenty of trees that were close enough for him to see. For some reason, this was his first time thinking about it, but he pulled his extended clip pistol from underneath his belt buckle and gripped it tightly in his hand.

Continuing to look around, he attempted to spot the person he had come to meet. After laying his eyes upon the same thing repeatedly, he was finally about to make his decision to head back to the car.

"Psss." That was before he heard someone calling out to him using the language they would use to get a dog's attention.

"Grrrrrr." The next sound he heard was a lower growl, which came from an actual dog.

Keem looked around once more without saying a single word. But the challenge to spot a body moving or standing still in the thick of the darkness was a grave one indeed.

"Over here." Keem then hears the whispers of a man's voice. Quickly, he attempts to turn around to catch the sound and match the voice with the person. All he came up with was another failed attempt.

"Spook, is that you?" Keem called out. "You really living up to your name already, my nigga. I'll give you that much. I just hope that your work is just as good as your introduction."

That was Keem's own way of introducing himself. He wasn't aware of what type of crazed maniac he'd agreed to go into business with. But soon he would find out.

Spook finally came from around the tree draped in a black trench coat that dropped down damn near to his ankles. To make matters worse, the palm of his hand gripped a leash that was attached to the collar of an all-black, full-grown large Bullmastiff dog.

The pet of Spook's sported a clear, bright white diamond-shaped spot right underneath its chest.

Keem stared at the animal directly in the eyes as the dog returned the favor with a growl.

"I hope you have control over your dog, brah." Keem warned as he gripped something in his palm himself.

"Diamond, down!" Spook commanded with the speech of only two words.

Before the last word was able to roll off Spook's tongue, Diamond's ass was already making its way to the ground. It was as if the pair were connected way past the point of verbal communication. They were able to speak a different language without even having to say a single word.

Spook walked a few inches closer to Keem, stepping into the moonlight. To Keem's unexplainable surprise, Spook was white. The expression of his thoughts was evident through his facial expression.

"Who sent you?" Spook questioned.

With only two short sentences, Keem was learning fast that Spook was a man of very few words, which was the first good sign in Keem's eyes.

"Mac." Keem's plan was to keep it short and as simple as the complicated man that he now stood before.

"Nice to meet you, Keem," Spook replied with the biggest sentence he's used throughout this short conversation. "I hear you've been having some sort of difficulty. My wishes are to take those small problems off your hands. I'm pretty sure that a man such as yourself has too many other issues to deal with to waste your time on roaches."

Keem paid close attention to the way Spook spoke. His words gave off a sense of a highly intelligent man with class. Plus, he didn't overlook the fact that he preferred humans to roaches. That statement alone spoke volumes within itself.

"You see, that's where I come in. Those same roaches that you want stepped on so badly, I consider to be legal tender. Now that we're in business, you'll learn soon enough exactly what I mean."

Reaching in the pocket of his trench coat, Spook pulled out a small business card and handed it over to Keem.

Out of confusion, Keem was hesitant to reach for the card. It wasn't something that was normal for him—knowing that Mac had already given Keem a card. That's what led him to this point.

But Keem was smart enough to know that when in Rome, you do as the Romans do. Keem took the card.

Simultaneously, as he searched for the right light to read the red words on the black card, Spook was explaining the reason for it.

"On this card is the location of our next meeting place. Now, being that you failed to follow the proper instructions prior to arriving here, which was to simply come alone, I heavily advise you to take heed to my demands the next meeting."

Keem's face grew slightly screwed for a few seconds for two reasons. One was due to the confusion of how in the hell he knew that Mia was waiting in the car. The second reason was because of the nerve of this nigga to demand who Keem decided to bring along to his happenings.

Eventually, Keem overthought his emotions and opened his ears.

"I grant you my understanding of your protection and safety, your business, and the decisions that you decide to make. However, the instructions I am providing for you are for those very same reasons. The only side proposal I have is to come alone or not come at all. And please do not think that you would be able to do so and get away with it without me knowing. Trust me, I will know."

Keem was at a loss for words. But then again, what was the point of exchanging words anyway, is what he concluded.

The man was loud and clear about the way he wanted to conduct business. But the point of meeting up here in the first place only to set up another meeting was extremely puzzling to Keem.

The interest Keem had in the strange man that he was just meeting was too high to describe. All he knew was that it was something that he wanted to figure out badly.

Was Spook's talk, or lack thereof, as good as the job he was about to be hired for?

The one thing that stopped Keem from doubting it was the fact that Mac was the one that advised him to give Spook a call and network. Soon, time would show Keem all he needed to see about the man that stood in his face at this very moment.

"Say less, my dude." Keem agreed to the conditions.

"Time?" Keem simply asked, quickly catching on to Spook's way of communications.

"You have the number." Spook simply replied. "You pick."

The next thing Keem knew, Spook was disappearing back off into the darkness as if he was never there in the first place.

"Everything good, bossman?" Mia asked Keem after he climbed back into the seat of the passenger side.

Keem, sitting there deep in thought and looking dumbfounded, was the reason for Mia's question.

"Keem!" she raised her voice a little louder.

"Yeah." Keem spoke nonchalantly, as if everything was perfectly fine. "It's some fucked up ass people in this world. And I thought I was fucked up. Let's get the fuck out this graveyard."

Lesson 3.10
Pay The Price

About a week after the attempted murder on Shy, he was finally able to be released from the hospital.

Now that he had gone through not only one but two near-death experiences within the span of a couple weeks, Shy's eyes were now wide open. He had that lock-in focus that some only dreamed of having.

The main thing on his mind—next to the revenge that he wanted to get on whoever the people were aiming to kill him and his brother—was the studio. He had written over a handful of songs while spending his time laid up in a hospital bed. So now, that's exactly where he was at, which was one of the first places he wanted to go once he was able to move on his own. The faint smell of weed and stale coffee hit him like home.

Although he was able to move around, it was very difficult for him to do it alone. One of his legs was still in major pain to the point that he could barely walk without the crutches that rested underneath his armpits. His head rung like the Liberty Bell on a continuous basis. He had about twelve stitches traveling halfway down the middle of his forehead from the cut that was once there. His back ached like the knee of an eighty-year-old man with arthritis.

But the worst pain of all lived in his heart.

With all the pain that Shy had endured throughout his life thus far, he thought that his biggest misfortunes were behind him. But the results from his recent encounters were enough to tear a man with average strength down to the size of an ant.

That wasn't the case for Shy. At one of the weakest moments in his life, he somehow found his greatest strength.

"Ayee, Tone, we gone take it from the top. I'ma run it again and then we can slap the hook in right after that part." Shy spoke through the microphone from the booth of the studio.

"Say less. Are you sure you are good on your feet? We don't have to rush through this shit. We can take all the time we need for real."

With the headphones over his ears, Shy was able to receive the response and question from Tone.

"Naw, I'm good. I need to get this shit out of my system while I'm really feeling it. Come on, let's run it." Shy assured with ambition expressing determination.

"Already, fool," Tone agreed reflectively. "If you need to take a break and sit down or something though, just let me know. Alright, let's go. We're taking it from the top."

Before Tone pressed the two buttons to rewind and record the song, he made sure to give Shy the proper heads up and warning, allowing him the time he needed to get his head back into the place that it needed to be.

"Ayee!" Shy began with an adlib before going in on the track with his brand-new verse, to his brand-new song.

***

After the last YNT shootout, Lil one's name has been ringing heavier in the streets. The way he's been moving, going hard for the gang every chance he gets, he was gaining stripes faster than his peers. Lil One was starting to be one of the most respected niggas in YNT. There was a time he almost got too deep in the mix, lost in all the mud they were stepping out of. But it felt good—real good—to have some solid ones to thug with. And the bankrolls he's been making just makes it even sweeter. Every stack he touched pulled him a little further from the official mission. He knew he had to stay focused. Keeping it together was one of his toughest challenges. Crow's murder consistently looped in Lil One's head; he used those terrible images to fuel his fire. If he let it slip, he'd be saying fuck the plan and fall off the deep end. Lately he'd been holding it down, so good he knew that one day the plan would be complete. When it popped off, Lil One would be satisfied and Crow would be able to get his peace as he rested. Lil One was determined to make it rained on BM's parade's before it was all said and done.

"Ayee, Lil One! Come on nigga! I'ma need you to ride with me. So, we could count this money up after we make this drop."

That was BM calling out, requesting Lil One to come on a ride along. That's just how comfortable BM was becoming with Lil One, wanting to keep him closer like he did all his soldiers whom he saw potential in.

Soon, they were both heading out the door and on their way.

Lesson 3.11
Stop The Hate

"Niggas be hatin', I ain't with the fakin' / I'm more like a lion, I step on these snakes / I send 'em to Zion, I'm droppin' that fire / I came with that heat, straight out the gates / Now niggas wanna stop me, good luck with that tryin' / They crossin' that line, it's the end of they race / Ain't with the violence, I swear I'm on peace / But if you try me, then you gon' meet your fate.

"So stop the hate... / Get on your grind, stop watchin' mine / And stop the hate... / Move at your pace, stop tryin' to race / And stop the hate... / STOP THE HATE!! Stop the hate. STOP THE HATE! Stop the hate."

A handful of YNT members were chillin' in one of the main apartments where they hustled, eyes locked on YouTube, watching the newest videos from local rappers. The current video on-screen—one of the hottest in the city, coming in just behind the artist's earlier hit—was Shy's newly released single, *"Stop the Hate."*

The main scene in the video was filmed in front of a tree near Hillside Court. Around the base of that tree sat teddy bears, flowers, vases filled with more flowers, posters, T-shirts, and balloons tied to strings that floated over the small memorial. That same spot had been an active murder scene just the day before. The brutal killing had drawn major attention across the city—it was savage, no doubt about it.

"Aye, whoever the motherfucker that did this shit is a cold son of a bitch!" The words flew out of Shoota's mouth like he wasn't a cold-blooded murderer himself.

"Yeah, I can't even believe a nigga done went that far to prove a point," Bank replied, shaking his head.

"Dead ass though. This shit here on some straight Ice Man type shit," Shoota added.

"More like KKK," Bank said. "No bullshit. The video fire as a bitch though."

A few of Shoota's boys chuckled at that, agreeing about the video. The others, though, were sick to their stomachs—couldn't wrap their heads around how somebody had the balls, the stomach, and the nerve to commit such a horrible act.

"Y'all niggas laughin', but I'll tell you one thing—whoever behind this shit, even a nigga like me would think twice 'bout fuckin' with 'em. They on some next-level type shit."

As those words left his mouth, Shoota paid attention to every one of them. The thought made him reflect. If seeing this type of shit made him feel the way he did, he could only imagine how everyone else felt. This was exactly the type of fear he wanted to place in his enemies. And to any other soul that dared to try their hands against his growing empire for that matter.

"This some wicked shit," he muttered quietly, before restarting the video from the beginning.

***

"Breaking news today coming live to you out of the Richmond area. Hillside Court is in a total state of shock as a young man was found hanging from a tree with a rope tied around his neck near the Hillside Court residence. The rope was tied into a noose, identical to the type of weapon that was used in the days of the slave era. Neither law officials nor the residents of Hillside Court can come up with an explanation as to why this happened, or even who could have done this evil deed for that matter. I am now going to hand it

over to our scene reporter, Samantha Oliver, who is on the scene right now as we speak. Sam, it's all yours."

"Hey, Kayla, thank you. Yes, I am here, unfortunately, on this very sad location of a young man losing his life, what seems to the naked eye to be out of pure hatred. Ironically though, the person responsible for this tragedy seems to be the very same person that's pushing a protest to stop the hate. As a sign was stapled to the young man's chest with the words reading as clear as day, 'Stop the Hate.' Now, no one in their right minds could figure out why this has happened in this way. Also, there seems to be not one witness available to point authorities in the right direction to a solid lead. Right now, there is not much we can inform the public about this incident, other than staying safe and being on the lookout for any information that we, or yourself, may be able to provide. Because I really believe that this will take a community effort to get this animal off the streets. Kayla, back to you."

"Whoever the nigga was that did that fuck ass shit deserves to get tow the fuck off. How the fuck you just gone hang a nigga like that, like they won't hanging niggas for hundreds of years?" Flex stood with his arms folded in front of the television, pondering on the latest breaking news, listening to the other inmates speculating on the topic. "Naw for real, that's some wild as shit." Most of the remarks were the same. "Ain't no way in Satan's hot hell is I'm going to even let a nigga get me in that position to be hanging from no mother fucking tree anyway." "Dead ass, like how the fuck was a nigga even able to pull that shit off."

"How y'all niggas so sure that it was even a nigga that did the shit?" Flex turned around to the crowd and asked a good enough question to silence the chatter. A few of the guys in the huddle looked around at each other waiting for someone to reply. It took a few long seconds, but eventually someone decided to speak up. "I mean unless you know something that we don't. Who else could it have been? You really think it was one of them white people that did something like this? And I know that might sound like a dumb question because they technically invented the shit. But you really think one of their asses gone step into Hillside just to pull out one nigga and hang his ass? Shit, all they have to do is just shoot the mother fucker like they do damn near every other day. And besides," the replied question from the man around the same age as Flex left him perplexed. So much so that he even went deeper into his thoughts about the situation. "I don't know," Flex started off by admitting that he was just as blind and lost as the rest of them. "One thing I can say whoever is behind this shit was definitely aiming to make a major statement. I ain't gone lie, this some fucked up shit. But it's one of the most gangster things I've seen in all my life. And trust me, I've seen some shit. But never some shit like this in my lifetime."

Flex was right. Someone was aiming to make a major statement, and to those who were the most accurate to their speculation, it was heard loud and clear. Not too long ago, Shy had what some may call a minor verbal altercation with a long-time neighbor from his hood. Ironically, it was during his last video shoot, which was also the first one he'd ever done. At the last scene of that video shoot, after Keem had pulled up to support in all the ways he could and then left just as fast as he showed up, a hater popped up from among the crowd thinking it was a bright idea to taunt Shy with his vicious words. The hater even went to the depths of sending silent threats on Shy's life. Eventually, gunshots had rung out, dispersing the crowd thin in every way which was able to spread. The first thing Shy did after escaping the video shoot that quickly turned into a crime scene was contact Keem and put him on game about the latest happenings.

Although Keem had already received the word about the disturbing events, he was extra vexed once he heard it come from the mouth of his baby brother. He was a protective person when it came to his people to start with. But when it came to Shy, he took the word overprotective and exaggerated it to its fullest extent. From there, Keem took matters into his own hands, taking the situation so seriously that he even informed Mac about the issue at hand. That's when Mac introduced Keem into Spook. The second meeting Keem had with Spook was when Keem gave the details of his first target that he wanted to eliminate. Keem wanted to send a message to all who were paying attention that he and his family was not to be fucked with in any way, shape, form, or fashion. Spook assured him that it would be loud and clear. But not even Keem would have thought that he would take the action to this degree. He may have felt a tad bit of disrespect but not a drop of disappointment. That was mainly because of the fact that Keem was giving Spook what he called a small test. The hater was lightweight in Keem's eyes. And before he sent Spook on the heavier mission that he had in mind for him, he wanted to make sure that he knew exactly what he was doing. And from this breaking news alert that had the city in a silent rage of anger, he was very pleased with the man's work.

Usually, Spook would conduct his business in a different matter. But after receiving the details from Keem and the reason behind why he wanted the hater erased, Spook formulated another plan in mind. He knew it would be risky, overjudged, and misunderstood even. He had no hate towards the young man. He didn't even know him to do so. He was merely doing a job that he was paid well to do. And being that Keem was a brand-new client of his, he wanted to make sure that he made this opportunity count, make sure that Keem would be satisfied with his work to the point that he'll return for more. With all of that being said, Spook purposely went overboard with his craftsmanship. The fact that he was the owner of his own morgue and funeral home made it extremely easy for him to get away with the crime of murder. All he would have to do is burn the bodies of his victims during the cremation process and just like that, a murder would be confused as a simple missing-person case.

Lesson 3.12
Be Careful What You Ask For
You May Receive

"Don't worry about it, partner. It shouldn't be long now. I know he'll be coming out soon. I've been watching him like a hawk, got all his moves down to a T. It's like playing chess with an opponent and they make the very same moves every game."

Calvez and Winchester had been stuffed up in a vehicle for almost two hours now, awaiting the arrival of Mac and his entourage. Calvez's obsession with Mac was growing bigger by the day. Winchester, on the other hand, wanted to focus on more tangible arrests and thought that booking Mac was a long shot away from today. He wanted to express that to his partner but felt it would be pointless.

"What about the lady that drowned in the river? And the two kids that we suspected to be the cause of it happening?" Winchester disregarded Calvez's comments and changed the subject to something that was more on his mind.

"What about them? One of the kids is dead, and the other is hiding for his life. We haven't seen him since the week after we picked him up for questioning. Besides, that woman was a well-known drug addict. Forensics labeled it an overdose before drowning." As Calvez spoke, he made sure to keep his eyes glued to the exit of the condo's main entrance and exit.

"Yeah, I guess you have a point. What about our words, though? You don't think that'll be enough? I mean, we did see her with our own eyes get into the vehicle with the two and follow them as they drove off. In fact, I think we'll have a much better chance of cracking that case than trying to build this—"

Soon enough, Winchester's words were being cut off by his partner's. The sad part about it was that it was right at the moment when he was about to speak up about the foolishness of chasing the mean, mad Mac.

"Alright, partner, saddle up. I think this is him and his team of convicts exiting the building as we speak now." As he spoke, Calvez started up the unmarked vehicle and waited until Mac and his team loaded the three newly released Mercedes-Benz G-Class SUVs. Calvez waited for about a speedy thirty seconds after the SUVs pulled off before he fell in line and followed them into traffic.

"Son of a bitch thinks he's so clever, changing up vehicles on the regular as if nobody's gonna notice three luxury cars back-to-back in this small-ass, raggedy-ass city of ours."

Calvez hated everything there was to hate about Mac, even down to the woman who birthed him. His entire career was built off just the thought alone of bringing Mac down to his knees. This was the bust he lived for. He thought about it every morning he woke up, every day he lived, with every second of breath he took. The day he'd finally be able to take Mac down might be the very same day he retired from his line of work. His mission would be complete—fulfilling his life's purpose.

"What the fuck are they doing now?" Calvez questioned, obviously vexed from what he was seeing with his eyes. The SUVs had come to a slow-moving pace right before pulling over into an abandoned parking lot only a few blocks from the condominiums they had just left.

"Looks like they're on to us, partner," Winchester assumed.

"That's impossible! It's been over ten years since I've been made. I'm one of the best stakeout detectives we have in this whole damn city." The ignorance of Calvez fooled him away from believing the fact that his partner just might be right.

"So, what do you think we should do?" Winchester asked a great question.

Calvez looked slightly over to the side where his partner sat in the passenger seat and replied, "Well, there's only one thing we can do from here. Go find out whether you're right or not, right?"

Winchester thought hard for a couple of seconds. "I'm not sure about that. We can play it off, you know, just keep it moving. Maybe save this activity for another day—a better day?"

By the time Winchester's words made it to the airspace of the car, Calvez was already pulling into the parking lot behind Mac and company.

Immediately as the car pulled up behind them, two men from the first car stepped out of the back seat as two men from the last car did the same simultaneously. All four men carried assault rifles of some kind in hand, with additional pistols hugging their waists for assurance.

Together, Calvez and Winchester hopped out of the car, waving their badges.

"RPD! Lower your weapons, NOW!" Calvez screamed at the top of his lungs. "And I am not going to say it twice!"

The men didn't move an inch. Before you knew it, one of the back passenger-side windows came down enough for Mac's top half of his face to be exposed.

"Y'all good. It ain't nobody but this faggot-ass nigga." He told his men to stand down. They lowered their weapons as they were ordered to do so—but only due to the orders of their boss and not the authority of the law.

Calmly on the outside, Calvez strolled his way toward the car that was parked in the middle of the other two, with the anticipation of approaching Mac.

"You know it's against the law for convicted felonies to bear arms in the state of Virginia, right, Mr. Macsby?"

Calvez asked as soon as he reached the halfway-open window of the middle vehicle. "And being that I know for a fact that you are a convict yourself, it's also illegal for not only you to be around other convicted felons, it's also against the law for you to be around all these weapons. That's even if you're not carrying, just in case you don't know—which I'm pretty sure you understand."

Mac eyed Calvez with a look that could kill. At first, he second-guessed his reasons for explaining himself to a lowlife such as the one he currently stared in the eyes of. Then he figured, what the hell—a murdered ego was the next best thing to a physical death.

"First of all, my men are legit as they come, unlike your crooked, boot-licking ass. They've never even seen the inside of a jail cell. Second of all, the vehicle that I occupy at this moment is as clean as my drawers. Now, if you don't believe me, you can take a whiff—right after explaining to me why you are always up my ass."

The comment pissed Calvez off to the point that he was speechless for a few seconds.

"For once, you're quiet." Mac lightly chuckled.

"Alright, that's it, smart ass. Get the fuck out of the car! Right fucking now!" Calvez demanded.

"Please don't do this, sir." Mac's words were more sarcastic than that of a plea. "I have a very important meeting to get to, and with the bullshit that you're on right now, you are sure to make me late. And I really don't think that's something that you would like to do. I am very precise about my business conductions."

"Is that a fucking threat, you asshole?"

By this time, Calvez was so infuriated with the nonchalance he was receiving from Mac that he got a grip on the door handle that Mac sat behind and took a very powerful pull at it in an attempt to open it. Unfortunately for him, the door was locked.

"You know, one of the easiest ways to get what you want in this world is to simply ask politely. Now, I may consider stepping out of this very comfortable position that I am sitting in if you can provide me with at least one legitimate reason as to why."

Mac was just as calm as an owl posted on the limb of a tree after midnight. Inside though, he was just as pissed off as Calvez was—if not more.

"You listen to me, you piece of shit, and listen well. If you do not comply with the orders that I'm giving you at this moment, I promise that you're only going to make it harder than it already is for you and the company you keep. I'm going to say this one more time, for the last time—get the fuck out the goddamn car right now before I blow a hole right in the middle of your fucking head!"

At this point, Calvez had reached the limit of the passes handed to him. Wisely, Mac drew up calculated plans in his mind, but he kept them in his own thoughts for obvious reasons. The tension felt like a breeze of air on a sunny day in spring.

A few eerie moments passed with the two men staring each other intensely in the eyes. If Mac's thoughts could be explained at that moment, it would resemble a scene directly out of a *Friday the 13th* movie—and Mac would be the star of the cast.

"Ayee, fellas!" Mac called out to his four men that stood outside of the car. "Y'all good," he said, relieving them of their current duty and preparing them to place their attention back on the business at hand. "Let's get the fuck out of here. This worrisome-ass pest ain't on shit. Nigga just trying to pluck my fucking nerves as usual."

By the end of his sentence, Mac had started to roll the window up in Calvez's face. Just before it was able to be sealed completely at the top, a hawk of spit came slipping through the crack, landing directly in the face of Mac.

"You son of a bitch! I didn't fucking dismiss you yet! Don't you ever fucking disrespect me like that again! You fucking do as I say at all times!"

Mac could hear Calvez vociferating right outside the car door. Humbly, he wiped his face and said, "Let's go. Pull off."

As always, his men did as they were told. The driver of Mac's vehicle honked the horn once to let the driver in front of him know that it was time to go.

As the trio of vehicles pulled off, Calvez was left standing there in a rage of anger.

"I swear on my fucking life, if it's the last thing I do on this fucking earth, I will make you regret every day you walked this earth! I'm going to make you hate your life so much that you'll wish you were a fucking fish in the sea instead! You hear me? You fucking hear me, Macsby?" Calvez shouted behind the rolling cars at the top of his lungs, badly wanting to be heard.

"You good, Bossman?" one of Mac's men asked from the shotgun seat position.

"Of course. Never better. The fact that I get under that bitch-ass nigga's skin so deep, and he still hasn't made a move, is all the confirmation I need to know just how untouchable we really are," was Mac's reply.

"True. But we don't take disrespect on any level from no one. So, do you want me to handle the situation for you?" the man asked, already willing to put his life on the line for the love and respect of his boss.

"Naw, you're good. I appreciate the gesture though. We need to keep our hands clean on this one. Give our friend a call, explain the details, and tell him we need it handled expeditiously. Remember, fellas—chess, not checkers."

***

"Anderson let's go! Your lawyer is here to see you."

Crawford released a button, deactivating the microphone that connected to each cell on the tier. Afterwards, she pressed another button, causing it to open one of the cell doors. Moments later, out strolled Flex, who was now making his way to the front of the tier towards Crawford.

"Boy, bring your ass on!" she said, half playfully and half seriously. "You always walking slow as hell like you Mr. GQ smooth or somebody. This ain't no damn runway."

"You said it, not me," Flex replied just as smooth as he walked.

Lightly, Crawford chuckled as she allowed Flex to walk ahead of her, leading them towards the doors to exit the tier. She used her key to unlock the doors one at a time before locking them behind her.

Their next destination was straight to the elevators, which were right in front of the 4E tier they had just left off.

"You ready?" Crawford simply asked while they waited for the doors of the elevator to open, without indicating exactly what it was that she was talking about.

"Yeah, hopefully her ass got some good news this time. It's been all bullshit so far, to be honest. I really can't trip for real, cause all that shit I did along with all the shit I got away with, I'm lucky to still even have a chance. But shawty a great fucking lawyer though. I've never seen a lawyer fight so fucking hard to help me beat a case in all my years of thuggin'. And you know what's even crazier? I've done some fucked up shit to her ass, and she's still putting up the best fight she can come up with trying to get a nigga from up under this shit."

Crawford allowed Flex to ramble on about his legal affairs while they stood in the hallway waiting for the elevator to arrive. It sounded as if he really needed to get that off his chest, releasing the pressure into the universe.

"Well, I hope everything goes good for you."

Ding!

The doors were sliding open the moment Crawford sent her regards toward Flex's legal battles.

"Something tells me that things will work out for the best. I hope so for your sake, at least."

Together the pair stepped onto the elevator.

"To be honest though, that wasn't exactly what I was asking about."

Flex stood staring straight ahead, watching as the doors closed on the hallway. He was trying to figure out what Crawford was actually asking him about.

The elevator ride down the few floors was a short and quiet ride. Right before the doors had an opportunity to draw open, Crawford was reaching out, touching the back of Flex's hand. The unexpected contact startled him. Quickly, he looked down towards where his hand was hanging by his side. At the same time, Crawford was placing the palm of her hand into his.

"He said," Crawford began, refraining from using any names for obvious reasons, "the first round is on you. Do what you do and get at him using the number that's in the package."

There now was a small package hidden in Flex's clutched fist.

"It's one hundred fifty in there. I don't have to tell you not to get caught with it, and if you do, what not to do."

Right before Flex was able to stash the package on his personal, the elevator doors were dinging open.

"Bet, say less. I know what time it is," Flex uttered so only Crawford and himself were able to hear his words. "It's time to run this bag up some more."

Crawford stood on the elevator, staring out at Flex as he headed towards the attorney's visitation area. She watched prideful as she thought about all the more money she was about to make through Flex.

She was proud that he was able to step up to the plate, taking on the challenge to carry the loads of their illegal business. Yet still, somewhere inside of her, she was cautious—hoping that Flex would not drop the ball and fuck up this wonderful opportunity of fortunes.

True enough, Crawford and E were cooking up plans of their own on the land to clean their illegal tender with a number of promising potential businesses. And although they had a stash full of cash to fund those businesses, Crawford knew that the money Flex could bring would be the guaranteed cash needed to stabilize the funding for everything that needed to be done.

Not to mention the extra money that they would gather from their partnership with Flex. And to her, that was one of the best parts of the cash flow—the fact that she was able to keep up with her business dealings while spending carelessly at the same time on the finest things of her liking.

For her, it couldn't get any better at this point. Things were going just as planned, if not better.

Only Crawford knew the trail and era, pain and torture, heartbreaks, and lonely nights she had been through—except for her. And with the story her life was giving at the moment, she would not mind keeping it that way at all.

But karmic law may have otherwise to say about that.

Lesson 3.13
Universal Law is Greater Than the Law

A little past the week after Calvez had that irrational altercation with Mac, he and Winchester were stopped at the light. The intersection was on Mosby Street. They were about to cross over from Littlepage Street and onto Fairmount Avenue.

"So, you really think after we snatch up little Macsby that'll bring out the big one?" Winchester asked, keeping his eyes on the street watching for any suspicious activity out of pure habit. The pair had just left the top of Mosby Projects in hopes of catching BM outside so they could harass and arrest him on any charge they could bring up, similar to how he tried to do Mac and failed horribly at. Calvez's plan was to go at BM as many times as he had to. Whether we was able to make bond or not, he would apply pressure until he nabbed BM on a charge that was able to stick, or it lured Mac out of his usual hiding, whichever one came first.

"Most likely not. He's a bastard himself. Piece of shit doesn't even give a shit about his own child. Shit, we will be doing the fuck face a favor by taking his son off the street. But what I was hoping for was that it would at least throw him off his game to the point that he takes a miscalculated step and slip off his game."

The light turned green. The vehicle drew to a slow roll to about ten miles per hour. Eventually seven more miles per hour were added, causing the car to creep at a speed of seventeen miles per hour. "This is an ongoing plan. If the first part of the plan isn't enough to get Macsby caught up in

73

the trap, then I'll round up hands full of people that's included in both of their circles, and put a bounty on little Macsby so they think he was the one telling on everyone that was caught up in the sweep. Hoping that someone would take the bait and go at little Macsby in attempts to take his head off. Now, I know that Macsby doesn't deal with his son at almost any level. But one thing I do know is that he hates his power to be tested. Just as soon as someone threatens to take a shot at something that has Macsby name on it, it'll cause an all-out war. And that will for sure throw Macsby off his game."

Except for two or three cars, Calvez and Winchester were the only vehicle on the Avenue of Fairmount at the time. "Well, hopefully, it doesn't have to come down to all of that and we'll be able to—" In the midst of Winchester's words, leading up to the end of his sentence, an all-black 2010 Dodge Challenger SE was slow creeping down the other side of the street. The windows on the vehicle were slightly tinted but deep enough to shield the vision of the driver away from pedestrians and other drivers nearby. Calvez waited a few hot seconds before encouraging his partner to continue.

"What was you saying? What's with the weird pause all of a sudden?" Winchester's hearing was impartial to both ears. Yet the words of his partner went into one ear and out of the other. Instead, most of his focus was on his sights and intuition. Everything about the suspicious car seemed innocent to the naked eye. It was the speed for Winchester, the all-around tint blocking the image of the driver. Also, something about the timing was off as well. Flicking on the flashing lights of the undercover detective police car, making a sharp U-turn, flagging the car, and stopping it, making sure that the person behind the wheel was not up to any wrong was the original idea that Winchester had in his imagination. After considering how outrageous the thought was, he quickly decided against it.

"Oh, nothing," Winchester continued, changing topics. "Just a thought."

The driver's window to the darkened Challenger suddenly came down just as slow as the car's speed. What happened afterwards was fast and swift, like a water snake snatching up a fish. A tan and black Banshee 300 MKG .45 ACP semi-automatic compact machine gun with an extended magazine was partially hanging out of the window before Winchester could even utter another word. Winchester cursed himself like a sinner repenting at Sunday's church service for the fourth time when he realized that he'd made the wrong decision.

Floc, Floc! The first two shots seemed to slow down the hands of time. All attention within earshot and eye shot of the firing weapon was now directed toward one way. For most it was a slight pause as they struggled to figure out exactly where the shots were coming from. Some made sure that they were not the targets of the day in this everyday warzone. Others hoped to prevent being the victim of an innocent murder. The two bullets penetrated the car on the driver's side door. The next round of shots accelerated the pace beyond normal. The total was five. A few bullets crashed into windows of the targeted vehicle, shattering them into thousands of pieces. At this time, the streets were in shock and chaos. People scrambled toward safety, screaming for their lives. Random shots rang out, causing side gun wars on the sidewalks closer to Mosby Court Projects.

"Partner! Get down!" Calvez ordered at the top of his lungs, snatching the pistol from his side and taking aim at the person in the vehicle that threatened to extinguish their lives. Winchester did as he was told, doing his best to support the wheel of the car with his eyes on the road from the crouching position. Calvez fired off as many shots as he could before the car completely passed theirs. As Winchester picked up speed to the moving vehicle, Calvez turned around in the passenger seat, now aiming at the back of the window. He let off a few more shots, shattering the back window himself in hopes of striking the predator or at least slowing him down.

Suddenly, the tires of the Challenger were squealing as the vehicle busted a U-turn so tight and quick that it caused smoke to arise from its wheels. "Go Chester, go!" Calvez was so anxious to get the words out of his mouth that he didn't even waste time calling Winchester by his whole name. Out of pure curiosity Winchester looked up into the rearview mirror that was now barely hanging from the top of the windshield. Noticing that this assassination attempt had just turned into a car chase, Winchester stomped the gas pedal to the floor, pushing the car up the small hill trying to put as much space between the cars as he could. Unfortunately for him and his partner, neither the Ford undercover police vehicle nor the operator, for that matter, was a match for the Challenger and the crazed maniac that controlled it.

The attacker rammed the front end of his car into the rear bumper of the car he chased down. The impact caused both Calvez and Winchester to jerk sharply following the motion of the car they rode in.

"Who the fuck is this asshole?" Calvez yelled over the chaos that could be heard all around him.

"I don't know!" Winchester yelled back. "You want me to pull the fuck over and ask him what the hell he wants?" The sarcastic reply pissed Calvez off to the point that he had to take his anger out on somebody. Gun in hand, he turned back toward the back of the car, lifted the pistol, and prepared to throw fire.

"Naw, fuck it. I'll find out myself. This lunatic is far from cordial."

As Calvez moved to execute his plan, Winchester thought of one of his own. Looking back into the rearview mirror he tried to see if the car was far enough behind them now that he would be able to see the license plate number. Before Calvez could even take a single shot, the car tapped into them again. This effect caused Winchester to take his eyes off focus. Even if he had the chance to look at the plates, he would have noticed that they were covered with dirt anyway and a long way from being readable. The Challenger was now picking up more speed and pulling up alongside Calvez and Winchester.

"Look out!" Winchester tried to yell before it was too late, being the one to catch what was about to happen. In an attempt to lighten the blow that was sure to come, he turned the steering wheel hard to the left, slamming into the side of the Challenger to throw the car off its balance and delay the inescapable.

With the passenger side window already down, the man in the car took aim with his weapon at the two detectives once more. Without hindrance he squeezed the trigger, unloading a load full of bullets into the car next to him. Behind the mask concealing his face, the man smiled noticing that the two were able to avoid the army of bullets that had just ambushed them. Quickly he accelerated the motion of the car and got out of dodge before he knew what was bound to happen.

As the Challenger escaped, Winchester's head banged into the steering wheel causing a forceful collision. As a result, he at once lost control of the vehicle, allowing it to swerve and slide from one side of the street to the other. The only luck the two detectives had at the moment was that there were not any other cars in motion for them to potentially collide with. Being that his body was already slumped over from the bullets that entered his side, the movement of the car forced Calvez to sway from right to left like a car dealership human figure balloon. Having this happen was a seemingly great thing because it was the reason he woke up.

Coming back from what could have been an internal slumber and placing him back in this moment in time,

Calvez cursed to himself, "Ahhh . . . fuck!" feeling the aching pains from the bullets while taking in everything that was happening right now. His side was burning like hot coal pressed against flesh. The sting made it hard for him to breathe, but the sight of the car fishtailing kept his focus sharp. Gritting his teeth, he pressed his left hand against his side, feeling the warmth of his own blood seeping through his shirt. Taking a deep breath to prevent panicking and making this tragic situation worse, Calvez thought fast about what he could do to get himself and his partner out of this bullshit of a mess. The first thing he thought of was figuring out why in the hell the car was swerving so loosely. Looking over to his left and noticing that his partner was out cold was logical reasoning to his questioning. Immediately he reached over as fast as his painful body would allow him and grabbed hold of the steering wheel. The jolt sent another wave of pain through his ribs, but he pushed through it. In an attempt to keep the car steady, Calvez freed up one of his hands so that he would be able to lift his partner's foot off the gas pedal. Each movement was like dragging a knife across his side, but the thought of crashing kept him conscious.

Afterwards, he scanned the streets for something that he could use to help slow down the car. Straight ahead of them was a roundabout with little to almost no traffic at all. A wise idea flashed into Calvez's brain and seconds later he was repeatedly beeping the horn trying to clear the path of anyone who might come close to crossing it. The fact that the car was already rolling uphill aided its slowing process. Once Calvez entered the roundabout, he stayed in it continuously until the car was down to a few miles per hour. His vision blurred for a second, the world threatening to tilt, but he forced himself to stay locked in. Soon afterwards he was able to pull it over to a nearby curb.

"Chester!" Calvez called out to his partner, landing heavy taps across his face, hoping to wake him. "Winchester! Come on, man, get up! We made it through. We're safe now."

Desperately, Calvez did all he could in the moment to wake his partner. "Shit," he cursed under his breath, fumbling for the vehicle's walkie-talkie so he could contact dispatch. "Umm, man down—shots fired." His voice cracked through the static, his hands trembling as the nerves throughout his body rattled every ounce of control he had left. "I repeat, man down. Shots fired. Come in, dispatch. This is Detective Calvez. I am hit, and my partner is down."

Hearing the words flowing out of his own mouth caused a tear to roll down his cheek. "Send medical assistance immediately! The location is Fairmount Ave and North 25th Street. Hurry, please!"

Pulling his blood-slicked hand away from his side, Calvez stared at the deep red coating his fingers. The pain was catching up now—sharp, pulsing, and cold. "I think I'm bleeding out," he whispered, his last words faint. His vision tunneled, the edges going black, and seconds later his body went limp in the passenger seat of the motionless vehicle, the frame riddled with too many bullet holes to count.

***

A couple days after E held up his end of the deal, which was passing the torch over to Flex, allowing him and Crawford to run the operation from inside, Flex came up with an even better way to return the favor. Even though E felt as if he was already indebted towards Flex for not just helping him with the elevation of his hustle but holding him down on the come up in many other ways, especially knowing that he had not a single obligation to do so. But the cream of the crop was Flex recommending that he hire Dawn Mornings as his lawyer. Even though the case was bogus from the get-go, E still felt as if not too many other lawyers would have fought as hard as Ms. Mornings did even with receiving payment. That was a connection that E would hold in his pocket for as long as Dawn decided to pursue her career in law. Not a bad idea on E's end considering the fact he was certain about the lifestyle he had chosen to continue in.

Speaking of connections, E pulled up into the Gilpin Court Projects in the Jackson Ward section of Richmond. He was there to meet a man that Flex had tied him in with. A man that E had heard of more than he'd seen. E wasn't surprised that Flex's networking had this level of reach. He just couldn't believe that his time had come to level up the standards of his own. While Crawford parked the car on Hickory Street down at the bottom of the projects, E made the call to alert his potentially new connection that he had arrived.

"Yeah, I see you," the man on the other end of the call confirmed. "Hop out right quick and pull up on me. I'm right across the street from you."

E put Crawford on game about his next couple moves even though he was unsure of what to expect next himself.

"You sure this is a good idea, Boo?" she asked a fair enough question. "I mean… I trust you, your decisions and all. But we don't know them. It's them I don't trust."

Crawford had a very valid point. The whole ride on the way here E was in his head trying to figure out for the life of him why in the hell would this man want him to meet in the middle of the projects out of all places. But nonetheless, it was his game, so it was fair to say E had to play by his rules. Mainly because this was an opportunity that he could not refuse, even if it meant taking the risk of falling into a trap. Luckily for E, the man he was meeting was not a man of that caliber and was excited to meet E just as much as E was to meet him. On top of all of that, for some reason, unlike others, E had some type of trust in Flex and doubted that he would send him on a dummy mission of disappointment. So, here they were.

E stepped out of the car and strolled across the street with confidence.

"You E, right?" the man asked for a slight assurance. "You must be expecting someone else too huh?" E's questionable response did not have a hint of sarcasm in it although the common mind would have mistaken it.

"Naw," the man replied, adding a light chuckle. "Business do be booming and all. But I don't usually move like this. I just had to make sure that you didn't have a problem with coming through the jects. Especially with you being from Mosby and all. Flex vouched heavy for you. But you don't have any beef with my young niggas out here or nothing like that, do you? I know the smoke heavy between y'all's generations."

Speaking of opps, E doubled-checked once more to see if he could spot any around, making this time more obvious than the last.

"At one point I did, but all that shit got cleared up when I was down in jail, for real. But you know how niggas is. You can never be too sure. That back door be wide open."

"Yeah, I understand completely. But look here," the man E was conversing with was none other than Brick himself, one of the most known unknown members of the 4 Horsemen of Richmond City. "You don't have to worry about none of that shit. Once you are on my team, it's all about that paper and my young people know and respect that."

E felt highly honored to be in Brick's presence. It was like a dream come true, like a child meeting his childhood hero for the first time. Of course, being from the other side of the tracks, and in addition to the fact that E was BM's best friend for as long as they could remember, Mac was the one E always envisioned himself working for. At this point though, working with Brick was just the same if not better.

"A'ight, now that's out the way, we can get down to business. Tomorrow morning six AM sharp and not a minute late, meet me down by the river at the beginning of the Canal Walk. There's a parking lot where the flood wall's gate is always open. That's where you'll make the pickup at. There's no need to bring any money and all that. Even though I've heard how strategic and strong your hustle is, I'm still going to try you out. This here is a whole different ball game. You may as well have a little experience and more. And I'm not doubting that. But with each level of the game comes a new set of lessons and tests. Also, you can thank Flex for the boost of my confidence in you. Yet again, seeing is believing. I know you've heard that one before. With that being said, I'ma hit you off with something small to start off with. And if you're a true hustler as the streets say you are then you'll be able to turn it up in no time."

"Already, that's a bet. Say less." It was E's reply after taking in all the instructions and advice that Brick had just laid on him. "Catch you in the AM then big dog. Let's turn this shit up another level." E reached his hand out and dapped Brick up once he did the same.

"Already, them the words I love to hear. If you have any questions or if anything comes up that might get in your way for any reason, you have my number so just hit my line. I keep it strictly business on that number though. Short, simple, and straight to the point. You good right?" The two newly made business partners released the grasp of each other's palms while respectfully keeping eye contact.

"Yeah, I'm good. I'ma go ahead and double-check to make sure my shit is ready for tomorrow. I dead ass didn't expect to meet a plug this fast. Especially not the best in the city."

Brick humbly chuckled at the complimenting fact. "Hey, sometimes it pays to know people. You feel me? Why do you think they call it a connect? But let me ask you something else though?" Brick was quick to move on from the topic at hand and get into a little more personal conversation.

"Yeah, what's that?" E wanted to know what was going through Brick's mind when it came to thoughts of himself.

"I've been dying to ask you this shit for real. And usually, I don't even be in people mix like this . . . but is that really shawty from the jail you got rolling round the city with you?" You could notice the excitement in every syllable of Brick's words.

Now it was E with the chuckles. "Yeah, man. Shawty through all green lights with a nigga. Ain't no telling how far she'll go." E tried to remain as humble as possible. But when the flooding thoughts of him bagging Crawford on top of the fact that he was standing here now receiving praise from one of his childhood idols made it even harder to hide the pride he felt for himself.

"Boy! You that mother fucking nigga, young nigga. A nigga like me ain't even pull no shit off like that before. I see you little nigga."

The two didn't notice it much but jealousy was beginning to thicken the air. Here was E, a former Mosby Court brave heart, and Brick, one of, if not the biggest drug distributors in the history of Jackson Ward, already a legend in about everyone's book who had knowledge of his existence, indulging in a conversation that exceeded the topic of just business. Some of the younger members from the projects didn't like the fact that Brick was becoming too close to E, so fast. For the ones that had it in their minds, this was a sign of the back door being close shut and locked.

"Okay, young nigga, I'ma let you slide. Plus, I have been out here too long my damn self. Remember what I said now. And if you need a nigga for anything as far as the business goes don't hesitate to hit my line. We're on the same team now. So, I guess that makes you my little partner or some shit like that." Brick chuckled once more, making the feelings of jealousy worse for those with weak emotions. "Keep doing your mother fucking thing, and I'ma help boss your status up for sure."

By this time Brick was already heading towards his vehicle.

"Already, I'ma make this shit count. You can bet everything on that."

From E's observation, Brick could hold a conversation like a candidate at a presidential debate. But when it was time for him to skate, he didn't play. Waiting not a single second of his time, on the move, still talking all the way up until the point his car had begun running. Wisely, E followed suit and figured he might as well get his ass out of here as well. His reasons for popping out were concluded. He felt as if there was no need to overstay his welcome.

"How did it go, Babe? Is everything okay?" Crawford was on the hunt for information as soon as E's ass hit the seat.

"Yeah, we locked in, Lil' Mama. Tomorrow morning, at six." E passed on the news. "Let's get the fuck up out of here before one of these hating-ass niggas try to pop up from out one of these cuts and I have to fuck somebody up out this bitch."

He didn't have to tell her twice. In fact, he didn't have to finish the whole sentence. Before he was even halfway through it, Crawford was putting the vehicle in reverse.

Now that E was in connection with Brick, things could be about to turn in the wrong direction for a few people — person of interest number one being BM. Not only was he still unaware of E's release, but now E had gained even more leverage on BM by gaining a plug of Brick's status. True enough, BM has a plug of his own — and a pretty good one at that. But BM was plugged in with Keem, who we all know works for Mac. If E can play his cards right and keep his hustle tight, then he'll be able to be in a similar position as Keem, placing him way ahead of BM on the food chain.

In addition to all that has to be considered, what about the Mosby Court Projects? How will they fare when everyone finds out for sure that E is actually home? And how will they feel when it comes to light that BM is a disloyal, betraying snake who came up off the pain, freedom, and near-death experience of the only nigga in the world crazy enough to befriend him?

Things are bound to make a major turnaround — the only question was how, and in whose favor?

Lesson 3.14
Go All In . . . Or Get Out

On the river of the Potomac, Shy and Destiny indulged in a tour cruise while they conversed about the happenings of their lives and what they expected of their futures. The boat traveled from the city of Alexandria, Virginia, and passed through Washington, D.C. In their sights were the most iconic landmarks of the city — the White House, Lincoln Memorial, Washington Monument, National Mall, Thomas Jefferson Memorial, United States Capitol, the Martin Luther King Jr. Memorial, and more.

"Shy." Destiny was staring out over the horizon of the waters, deep in her thoughts.

"What's up, Des? What's on your mind?" Shy moved closer toward her, wrapping his arm around her waist and placing a soft kiss on the nape of her neck.

"I really hope, after all you've been through these past few weeks, that you learn to move a little more cautiously when you get back home."

"Huh?" Shy questioned her, misunderstanding at first. "Exactly what are you saying?"

It wasn't that he didn't get the point Destiny was trying to make — it was just that, in his world, Shy was one of the most cautious people he knew. In his eyes, he couldn't get any more careful.

"What I mean is that you have so much potential. You're a person with a wonderful and beautiful heart. You take your life to places that most of the people you live around could only dream of — if they could even think that far. To be honest with you, Shy, the more I'm around you, the clearer I can see you. When I first met you, I did something I rarely do — I judged a book by its cover. I expected you to be a certain way because of how you looked. And then you spoke...and I knew with your first few sentences that you were someone worth getting to know. Someone underestimated. Someone who could give my life more purpose than just a school scholarship and a career. Now that I feel myself getting so attached to you, I can't feel myself without you. I don't want to have to move on in this life without you. If something was to happen to you, I don't know what I'd do. I've never allowed a person to get this close to me. It took me years to let someone in since the passing of my father. Ever since he was murdered, I've looked for him in every man I'd so much as hold a conversation with. If I didn't see him in a man within the first few seconds, I'd fabricate an escape.

"That's not the case with you, Shy. You are the man I've been looking for in every man. You're the one I want to hold my hand day in and day out. Do you know how many times I've thought about dropping school lately just so I could be by your side every second of the day? But one thing I don't want to do is give my life to someone who's giving theirs to the streets. Especially when I know for a fact you've got so much potential. The streets took my father away from me, and he loved me with everything he had — every bone in his body. Swore everything he was doing; he did for me. When all I wanted was for him to be here now."

Shy's arms traveled from around Destiny's waist, stopping just under her breast. The grip tightened as he hugged her with passion. For the moment, all he could do was embrace her as her words bounced through his brain, back and forth between his conscious and subconscious.

After allowing himself a few seconds to register the sincere feelings behind Destiny's words, Shy contemplated the perfect response.

"For one, you're not dropping out of school — not for me or anyone else. You only have a little over a year left before one of your biggest dreams comes true. I love that you're so concerned about my safety, but I need you to know I'm fully protected — more than you know. Even that last attempt was a desperate move by the opposition, something only a checkers player would make. And baby, even if I was a player in the game, I'd definitely be a chess player — and I'm not talking about being a pawn either.

"Remember our first date? We had such a good time that you made me forget all my worries back then. You had me sitting at the top of the world, and I barely knew you. Then all that chaos popped off as soon as we walked out the doors. In order to protect my people — which was actually you and your people, a few folks I'd just gotten to know at the time, I may remind you — I felt it was my job to protect y'all and myself at all costs. You saw firsthand the lengths I'd go for someone I'd just met. So, I'm pretty sure you can imagine how far I'd go for someone I've loved all my life. And trust me, it's like that because them same people I'd put it all on the line for, they're willing to take it even further for me.

"I have a lot of good luck because, yeah, I'm a good person and I do as much good as I can for everybody I meet. But I'm also smart. You said it yourself — I'm underestimated all the time. Most of them niggas out there can't pinpoint how I'm coming, when I'm coming, or even if I'm coming.

"But if it makes you feel any better, my big brother won't even let me get in the game. Like you, he expects so much more out of me that he'd strangle me himself if he knew I was doing something I had no business doing. Especially after he found out how good I can rap. He sees all these people fuckin' with me, spent all this money investing in his own studio, and now he's confident I can be the one to get us out of this fucked-up lifestyle. And all I've ever wanted was to make him proud. Now that I have that chance, I can't let him — or myself — down.

"In addition to all that, I got you now — someone who sees me for who I am. I don't have to worry about making you proud, because it's like you already are. Even if it's just me trying to be the best I can be. Since I've met you, you've been cheering me on the whole way. Believe me when I tell you, I got you. I'll do what I have to do to keep myself safe and living. I promise, I won't let a soul on this earth take me away from your love."

Shy did his best to convince Destiny that she was overthinking his situation. But truth was, even he wasn't sure what to expect next. His biggest concern was his limited knowledge of the people who'd tried to take his life — and his only partial understanding of their motives. It was known that Shy took one of their men out of the game, but that had been only to protect his brother. Before that, he knew nothing about the threat whatsoever. Hell, not even Keem could've seen it coming, even if it was right across the street.

One thing Shy was sure of, though, was that he refused to go out like a sitting duck. He was also pretty sure Keem would strike as fast as lightning before the enemy could make another attempt on either of their lives. For now, he'd settle for telling Destiny a couple harmless little white lies just to keep her mind at ease — so she could focus on what's important in her life while he did the same in his.

What Shy didn't know, though, was that before Destiny dealt with another heartbreak — losing another man she loved to the streets — she'd rather leave Shy behind and move forward with her life. She viewed their relationship as requiring complete commitment. Partial involvement, in her eyes, didn't count as genuine love.

"I hear you, Shy, and I understand. I just hope you mean every word you're saying — and that you pay close attention to what I say, and how I feel about these things. Everything we do comes at a cost. Sometimes, we don't realize how it'll affect the people we love until it's too late . . . even if it's unintentional."

***

"This is hands down one of my favorite restaurants. I absolutely love the menu here, and the staff is also so nice to me."

Leilani, accompanied by Mac, was being guided to their seats. They settled on the balcony of The Boat House restaurant that sat on the bank of the James River.

"You must leave big tips all the time then, huh?" Mac lightly and politely joked while pulling out the chair to allow his date to sit.

"No," Leilani joked back, sporting a beautiful, blushing smile. "But I do leave enough to express my gratitude."

Mac walked around to the other end of the table and settled into his awaiting seat. "Oh, and we both know just how grateful you are about everything!" There was emphasis on the word *everything*, Mac using sarcasm to draw another smile across her face.

"And that's why I'm so blessed. Thank you very much. Always trying to be funny. You should try it." She shot back with the voice of a flirtatious high school teenager.

"It got you smiling, so my funny attempts must be of some success. And I am grateful. I'm grateful for a lot of things. Just because you don't notice me expressing it doesn't mean that I don't do it."

Minus the hard feelings, Mac defended himself.

"Oh yeah? Well, name one thing you're grateful for." Leilani decided to challenge him.

"You," Mac shot back into the atmosphere without hesitation and full of confidence.

"Me?" Leilani asked, disbelief written all over her face. "You mean to tell me out of everything you could be grateful for, the first thing that comes to your mind is me? Little old me? A man that damn near has it all?"

It wasn't that she didn't feel like someone worth being grateful for—it was just that she hadn't expected Mac to say, *her*, out of all things.

"First of all, you're not old. You're seasoned and as healthy as you can be. Second, I nearly had it all before I met you. Now that you're here, I can officially say I have it all. I thought things were going well before we met, but afterwards, I realized that something had been missing the entire time. Since you've been in my life, you've helped me realize that I'm actually a very blessed man. You help me shift my attitude toward gratitude with all your meditations and all that other crazy stuff you have me trying out—"

They both shared a moment of laughter.

"Nah, really though, I've been feeling like a brand-new man since you walked into my life. Every moment I get to spend with you is cherished to the fullest extent of my gratitude. I can just picture all that we might achieve and experience together."

The waiter approached the table to take their orders. They requested a couple of glasses of water; Mac ordered one of his favorite alcoholic beverages, while Leilani settled for a glass of wine. They both agreed on an appetizer and asked the waiter for a few more moments to decide on their main dishes.

They already knew what they were getting.

Mac, being the gentleman that he was, refused to order before his lady. On the other hand, Leilani was so wrapped up in the conversation that food was the furthest thing from her mind.

"So, exactly what type of plans did you have for us?" Arms folded, she leaned back in her chair and stared directly into Mac's dark brown eyes.

Matching her stare, Mac searched his mind for the perfect answer. For the first few seconds, he wondered what exactly she wanted to hear. Truth be told, there were quite a few things he wanted to tell her. But for prideful—and even understandable—reasons, he decided it was still too soon to reveal such deep expectations and goals for their newly sprouting relationship.

Although, there was one thing in particular he felt could no longer wait. It was the main reason they were both seated here now in this beautiful place of dining, having such a wonderful time with one another.

As a man of calculated scheduling, he felt as if he'd already wasted enough time on the mission at hand. Even his business partners had begun to question if he was the right man for the job at this point. They all predicted that Mac would surely have received an answer by now, when truly, he had yet to even scratch the surface of presenting the business proposal to Leilani.

The more time they spent together, the harder it became for Mac to pop the question. Unlike his usual self, he'd gotten too far away from the business aspect of their relationship, placing more focus on building a personal one. At times, he even told little white lies to himself, convincing his own mind that it was all part of the plan—which it had been, in the beginning. But now, he wasn't so sure.

It almost felt like he was about to ask for the woman's hand in marriage and was too nervous to go through with it.

But since she had just asked the question at hand, he figured—when better than now?

The last thing he wanted was for her to find out that all their time spent together had been built on a lie—a scheming plot to use her name in a game of chess to advance his financial goals. He knew her response would be either yes or no, and it would all depend on how he presented the idea.

"Well," Mac began slowly, still figuring out the best way to say what needed to be said. "With all the greatness and potential that you have, I really see us accomplishing a great deal of things together."

He turned his Mac all the way up, smoothing his voice even more than usual.

"You know, you speak a lot about this universal talk, right? And I find it crazy that you showed up in my life at the exact time you did. Even the way we met—it was confirmation, an answer to this grand plan I've been dreaming of carrying out for years now.

"Apart from being so wrapped up in the complexity of your personality—the intriguing thoughts and ideas of your mind, the loving, warm, and comforting feeling of your heart, diving into the depths of your soul, and the amazing admiration of your beauty—I haven't really had the time to think about anything other than you. Especially when you're in my presence.

"I mean, don't get me wrong. You know by now that I'm a man of business. So, when we're apart, I do my best to stay focused on the task at hand without letting my mind wander to thoughts of you. Sometimes I win. Sometimes I lose. But either way, it's a win—because just the thought of you gives me the motivation to strive.

"Ever since I've gotten to know you, you've been the solution to all my problems. When things get stressful or frustrating, I think of you, and you bring me peace. When I feel my temper rising and I'm about to be angry, the thought of you calms me. If I feel like I'm getting off track, you remind me that I'm right 'where I'm supposed to be in this exact moment.'"

Leilani finished the last few words along with him—it was a quote he'd picked up from her on one of their late-night calls. She smiled, pleased that Mac had been listening to the advice she'd shared through their conversations.

"Another thing that wrecks my brain whenever we part ways is why in the hell didn't I just ask her? And that same thought is what washes all my doubts away. I think I was meant to meet her; this isn't by chance. This is destiny—it was meant to be.

"I just don't know how to present it to you for some reason. And it's not because I didn't do my homework or know every detail of the aspect. I really think it's because it's been a long time since I've been this deep in intimacy—and I've never done business with an intimate partner before. I'm a whole different monster on that level, and—"

"...And I can't see what's so hard about you just saying what it is you need to say. You know, up until this point, you've never given me the impression of someone who bites his tongue. I think the best solution is for you to just spit it out, or let's change the subject, because the anticipation is killing me softly."

Leilani dragged out her last few words with a playful drawl, wrapping her arms around her shoulders and tugging them lightly.

Mac released a short chuckle as he glared at her for a moment, caught off guard by the confidence she'd just sparked in him.

"You know what?" Mac interlocked his fingers and rested his forearms on the table. "You're absolutely right. I just hope you're ready for this—because it's an earful."

He paused again to gauge her reaction. She was unfazed, still waiting for the big announcement.

"I want to open a bank."

The two stared at each other, eyes locked, not a blink or hint of movement between them.

"That's it?" Leilani asked, disbelief coloring her tone. Up until this point, she'd been certain Mac was a man who already had an active bank account. But if not, then her suspicions about him being a major drug lord might've just been confirmed.

"Yeah," Mac replied nonchalantly, slightly confused.

"You say it like it's something that's just that easy to do or something." The look on Mac's face said it all.

"So, you're really sitting here telling me that you don't have an open bank account by now? And you're how old again?" Now Leilani was the one confused.

"Ohh…" Mac released a chuckle that made Leilani frown a bit. "I get it—we're having a little miscommunication issue here," he explained.

"Okay, please explain," Leilani urged.

"I want to open a bank—as in, my *own* branch. Like a building full of money, crypto options, the whole nine, and whatever else comes with it." Mac did his best to simplify exactly what he meant down to full understanding.

"Ooohhh… now I get it. I see what's going on here. Well, first of all, let me start by saying that it is a very strenuous goal. I'm not saying that it's impossible, because obviously a handful of people have made it happen before. Me knowing you the way I think I may"—the way she pronounced the word *think* was as if she were unsure about what she was saying out of her own mouth—"I conclude that you are the type of man that goes after what he wants with all that he has in him and will not stop by any means until he reaches his objective. That's understandable. I respect and absolutely love that about you.

"But I have two simple questions for you. How do you plan on getting this done? And exactly what do I have to do with this major dream of yours?"

Now that the ice was broken on the question, Mac felt more comfortable speaking on the topic and went straight into the details of his understanding.

"Those are a couple of great questions. First of all, I've done an exclusive amount of homework on the project and have even taken the first few steps toward making this dream of mines a tangible reality. Now, where the idea of you comes in, there's something called a *bank charter* that I'll need to provide for the OCC—that's the Office of the Comptroller of the Currency.

"A bank charter is a person who has a strong background and can be the face of the bank. As for the deeper details, I'll be able to provide that for you as well. Obviously, there's no need to if you're not interested from the beginning."

"Oh, this is all so very interesting. But now I have another question. It may seem rhetorical, but can you simply explain to me the reasons as to why you can't be the face of your own bank?"

Mac thought of the best and easiest way to answer the question before responding.

"Well, if I may be honest with you, I don't have one of the cleanest criminal records. I have a past—"

"As we all do. Apologies, please continue." Leilani interjected briefly before allowing Mac to move on with his explanation.

"And in that past, I was a much more ignorant man—meaner, and a little bit riskier. So, I found myself in some trouble a few times. Which is the thing that's now holding me back from making a couple of the moves I wish to make. This being one of the main ones."

Leilani held a deeply thoughtful expression upon her face, contemplating the best angle to approach this current situation. While she did so, Mac sat by, wrecking his own brain about the thoughts she could be having. There was one thing he knew for sure: he would be one step closer to his plan regardless.

Whether she agreed to move forward with it or not, he'd know exactly what he needed to do from here.

"Okay, so here's what I think we should do," Leilani started, finally breaking the silence in the conversation. "First of all, I'm not the one to judge people for the mistakes they've made. However, I do note the way they react to them after the fact. Clearly, you've successfully made a major recovery from whatever trials and tribulations you've had to deal with in the past.

"Also, I'm a firm believer in giving a helping hand to people receiving second chances in this game of life that we all play a part in.

"As far as this banking business you speak of, I would consider it only after further deliberation of exactly what it is that my name will be attached to. I've worked extremely hard to keep my name clean while dealing with my fair share of dirt balls. Not saying that you're one of them, but moving further along with this mission, you never know who we might have to make connections with, in order to get to where we're trying to go.

"Sad to say, but it's just the world we live in. Seeing that I don't feel like this is a suitable time to be discussing business—along with the fact that we should be enjoying each other's company right now—I'll get back with you on that topic soon. But until then, have you ever heard of an expungement process?"

To say the least, Mac was in total shock at how easy-going this woman was. To be honest, he hadn't expected her to be so open to the idea. Actually, he thought she'd shut it down as soon as the words left his mouth.

But not only had she considered it, she was now sitting here convincing him—informally, at that—how to get his record clean altogether.

Mac had met a lot of women in his many days, but never one such as this. He was a businessman, hands down—a man who led with his mind instead of his heart.

But lately, he'd been feeling something in his chest that he hadn't felt in a very long time.

Lesson 3.15
More Money, More Problems

The morning after meeting Brick in the projects of Jackson Ward, E arrived at the location he was told to be at—ten minutes early. Although he expected to meet Brick himself for the second time, it was an unknown man who passed him a small bag holding the brick inside. E was ready to break it down, cook it up, cut it up, and bag it. He intended to move it all on his own. Besides, he had to—at the moment, he didn't have a team to avail oneself of.

His plan was already well put together in his head. With all this work on consignment, his goal was to whip up the best coke in the city, wiping out the competition and letting the fiends know that spending their money with him would be worth their while.

Before heading to their next destination, E directed Tiara to stop over at his grandmother's house, found at the bottom of Mosby Court. There was something he wanted to pick up—something he didn't feel right moving around without. Plus, he figured he should go and see his grandmother, let her know he was well and okay.

Thinking a couple moves ahead of the opposition, E figured that at this time in the morning, mostly everyone would be tucked away in their apartments. So, he'd run only a slight risk of being seen by anyone. Using the key, he kept on him at all times, he crept through the front door with Crawford right behind him.

"Lock the door," he demanded, flicking on the light switch to remove the darkness from the kitchen. Afterwards, he headed toward the living room to check if his grandmother was on the couch. By now she'd usually be up, sipping her coffee and tuned into the news.

"She must not be up yet," he said to Tiara. "You can come in here and sit down. I'ma just run upstairs, grab something real quick, say hi to my grandma, and then we out."

Before doing as he said, E handed Tiara the remote to the television. "Make yourself at home." Then he lightly jogged up the stairs.

Not even a minute after E disappeared to the second floor, the lock on the back door was being unfastened again. The rattling startled Tiara for obvious reasons. Although she was smart enough to figure that if someone had a key, it must be someone who lived there or was trusted with access, the way E talked about people from his neighborhood taught her not to trust *anything*, regardless of how it seemed.

She thought to herself: *What should I do? Should I yell for E, make him think I'm in danger and risk both sides reacting wrong? Or just sit tight and see what happens?*

"Damn, who the fuck is you?"

Before she could decide, a man came around the kitchen corner into the living room. "I mean, you bad as a motherfucker and all that, but how the hell you get up in my shit? BM sent you here, didn't he? Left a little present for a nigga? That slick-ass nigga! How the fuck he pull this one off? I know for a fact Granny ain't go for this shit that easy. That nigga must've paid my old lady off to turn a blind eye."

By the time Tru was done running his mouth, E was jogging back down the steps. The sound of quick feet made Tru nervous—he pulled a pistol from under his coat.

"What the fuck?" was all he managed as he aimed the gun.

E stopped at the bottom of the steps, took three seconds to assess the situation, and said, "Little nigga, stop aiming that fucking gun at me before I beat your ass. You ain't gon' shoot that bitch anyway."

E was already moving as he finished his sentence. He walked over to Tiara and grabbed her left hand as she sat on the couch. "You good, boo? This little nigga ain't fuck with you, did he?"

"Yeah, babe, I'm straight. And naw, he's good. You ready to go?"

Before answering, E turned to face Tru, who stood frozen, still stunned by his older cousin's presence. Tru could barely believe what he was seeing. He thought he was tripping— maybe sleepwalking or stuck in some vivid dream.

"I need to holla at this little nigga right here anyway," E said. "Glad I ran into him. Bittersweet, I guess." He looked Tru dead in the eyes.

Tru could feel the energy between them but had no idea where it came from. "Damn, cuz, what's happening? I ain't know you was home! When the fuck you touch down? Why the fuck you ain't put niggas up on game? You know damn well we would have rolled out the red carpet for a real nigga like you. I know you heard by now, but we havin' our way in these streets—straight runnin' shit out this motherfucker. And BM put this whole shit together, so you know your spot locked in, for sure."

The deadly silence from E's reply made those few seconds feel like minutes. When he finally spoke, his tone made the reunion even stranger.

"Did you ever stop to ask yourself why I didn't call as much as you expected me to? Or wonder why you never heard me ring that fuck nigga's line? Why he never mentions me to you? I'm pretty sure he didn't. You never thought, not once, that something wasn't right?"

E paused again—but not to give Tru a chance to answer. He was reading his body language, knowing it would tell him more than words ever could.

"I know you didn't," he said flatly. "And that's part of the reason I'm giving you the benefit of the doubt—and a chance at redemption."

"Redemption?" Tru mumbled under his breath, confused.

"Yeah, nigga. Redemption." E shot back, fast, as if he was a gunslinger. "Cause see, here's the thing you don't know—you done fucked around and got yourself stuck in the middle of some shit. You're out here siding with the opps. When I first heard you was rocking with that nigga, it pissed me off to the point I couldn't sleep for days.

"The first thing I thought was, how the fuck could my own blood cross me for my own nigga? I was the one who raised you, kept you fed when your mama chose the streets over her own son, when Grandma was sick and couldn't. I was the one there for you—always. No matter what.

"But then I reminded myself—no one knows about the shit that went down between me and dude. That's when I realized you just a blind, young, dumb-ass nigga following another. I bet your mind racing right now, right along with your heart.

"In case you wonderin', I left your ass in the dark for a reason. I wanted to see where your loyalty really lay. Aside from that, by now you should know everything I need to know to help me achieve my mission."

Tru's confusion was through the roof. "Cuz, what the fuck are you talking about?"

"Nigga, shut the fuck up!" E's temper went from bottled up rage to almost being untamed. "I ain't ask you to say shit! And when I do, you better hope you say the right motherfucking words."

"Yeah, but you in here actin' like you wanna take something out on me when I don't even know what the fuck going—"

If Tru's mouth ever got him in trouble, now was one of those times.

E whipped out what he'd come to the apartment for in the first place—though he hadn't expected to use it so soon. With the speed of a buzzing bee, pistol in hand, he swung and cracked Tru across the head.

Tru stumbled. E grabbed his throat with his free hand, slamming him back against the concrete wall.

"Listen, you little bitch, I'm already tired of fucking talking!" Spit flew from E's mouth as he clenched his teeth. His voice was the angriest both Tru and Tiara had ever heard. They'd only known the loving side of E—until now.

"You don't know half the shit I been through this past year. And I ain't got time to explain it. Just know this—I got enough built up in me to kill that bitch-ass nigga BM and anybody rolling with him. I'll tear down everything that nigga built—piece by motherfucking piece, or all at once. I don't give a fuck, as long as I get to see it crumble by my own hands."

"Now, like I was saying..."

E eased up on Tru—just enough for him to see what condition he'd put him in. Blood dripped from the corner of Tru's lip. His eyes were wide, fingers trembling.

"I don't give a fuck what you do," E continued. "Just know that once you pick a side, your ass gon' stay there— and eventually lay there if it ain't over here where I stand. Whatever you decide, I want you to go back, keep playin' your part, and do exactly what you've been doing. I'ma text you. In a couple days, I'll be expecting to hear something back. If I don't, I'm gon' assume you decided to keep your disloyal ass over there, even after I took the blindfold off your eyes. Do I make myself clear?"

"Yeah, but damn cuz, you coulda just said all that without tryna fuck a nigga up."

Tru had a point—except for one thing.

"You talk too damn much," E said. "That's your fucking problem. You so spoiled, you think just 'cause you my cousin, you can run your mouth, and nobody'll touch you. Then you talk slick to me, like I won't fuck your ass up. Let this be a warning—you dead wrong if that's what you think. This situation too serious to trust anybody who ain't rockin' with me a hundred percent."

E lowered the gun and backed off. "You heard what I said. I hope you got the message loud and clear. Don't fuck around and take too long to make up your mind—even though this shit should be a no-brainer."

"Come on, cuz, you already know how I'm rocking fool."

"Yeah, alright, we gone see."

"But what about that nigga BM?"

"What about him?"

"Do you want me to tell him you home, or keep the shit on the low?"

"Like I told you, I don't give a fuck what you do or how you do it. Either way it goes, nigga ain't gone be able to stop shit I got coming his way. And nigga I put that shit on your life. Come on Boo, let's get the fuck out of here."

***

"Nigga, where the fuck your little bitch ass been all motherfucking day?"

BM and the rest of the YNT members were posted up around the table in the kitchen, where they held most of their meetings.

"You was gon' be mad as a bitch if you'd missed this breakdown. Shidd, you know I don't mind keeping a little extra work for myself."

Almost six hours after his encounter with his cousin E, Tru was now walking into the YNT trap house. He'd spent those few hours wrecking his brain, trying to figure out what in God's green earth was going on between E and BM. For as long as he could remember, the two of them had always been best friends. From the outside looking in, Tru had never noticed any type of conflict between them whatsoever.

Now, all of a sudden, E was talking about murdering BM.

All Tru's young life, he'd wanted to be part of their circle. He loved his cousin to death and hated whenever E or BM excluded him from their criminal activities. So, the moment

Tru finally got a chance to be part of something BM had built, he was all for it. It was something he'd been preparing for his whole life. The only thing missing was for E to come home so the three of them could run things together. Tru finally had a reason for living.

"Mane, my ass was tired as a bitch for real," Tru said. "Nigga hit three all-nighters back-to-back. Shit caught up with me this morning when I hit Granny's crib—especially after I hopped out of the shower. It was a wrap."

"Uh-huh, whatever," BM replied. "You the one that missed out on all that paper. Shit was jumpin' this morning out this bitch."

"Shit ain't bout none, for real. I'ma make it up anyway." Tru rested his back against the countertop.

"Yeah, I know you better—before a nigga snatch some shit out your cut." BM was counting a handful of money with the help of a few other semi-trusted members.

"I always get mine, and some more," Tru shot back, tired of being taken for granted. He loved, respected, and looked up to BM—but he was over being a pushover. "Plus, niggas got way bigger problems to worry about than bitchin' over that."

While he'd been thinking all morning, one thing crossed Tru's mind—he had BM's life right in the palm of his hands. If BM didn't want him to metaphorically close his fist and end it, then BM would have to earn it. Starting by treating Tru with more respect.

At that moment, Tru was undecided, but he knew one thing: he had to get to the bottom of the situation. There was only one way to do that.

"I gotta put you on game about some shit," he said finally.

BM hesitated mid-count, pausing for half a second. "Brah, ain't nobody worried about that shit you talkin' about. Niggas tryna get this money straight. You with it or naw?"

Before responding, Tru took a long minute to think. "Naw, brah. I think you need to hear this shit."

The tone in Tru's voice made BM think twice about brushing him off.

"A'ight, nigga, spit it out already. Sound like you really need to get that shit off your chest."

Tru took a deep breath before letting it all out—without knowing or even considering what could come behind it. Honestly, he just wanted clarity for himself.

"Yeah, well . . . I don't know if you wanna hear this, 'cause I'm pretty sure you got no idea. But my cousin E just came home. And to be honest, the nigga giving sneaky vibes. I don't know how long he been home, but he out this bitch—and I figured I should put you on game. On some heads-up type shit."

A few bills slipped from BM's hands, falling onto the table as his mouth hung open from the news. He'd figured the day would come—but he'd hoped it would be years from now, maybe even a decade.

Now, he didn't know what to think. His mind went blank, trying to process the words that had just hit his ears.

Brah, what the fuck? I can't let this shit happen. I know for a fact that nigga E got something up his sleeve. I need to figure out how to stop whatever he got planned—'cause I know he know what's up by now. He's smart enough to piece this shit together.

And I need to see what's up with Tru. Ain't no telling what he told E. Nigga could be rocking with us just to feed dude info—on some inside shit. I can't even lie, though, this shit is about to get real, as if it wasn't real enough already. I don't give a fuck. I'm ready for whatever. If a nigga can't bet on nothing else, he can bet on that.

So many thoughts ran through BM's head that he couldn't explain them even with a dictionary. He barely had a reply to the news he'd just received. All he could manage was:

"Aight, so why you actin' like that's bad news or somethin'? Shit, my nigga home—we about to turn this bitch up for real, for real now."

The look on Tru's face was priceless. Aside from the disrespect he felt from BM, he was almost tickled to his core that BM was playing his role perfectly. Now, knowing what he knew, Tru could see right through BM's tactics—and that placed him a move or two ahead on the chessboard. He was smart enough to use that to his advantage.

"Yeah, that's a lock. We most definitely about to turn the fuck up! My motherfucking cousin home! He out this bitch—shit about to really get real!"

Tru's excitement was too much for BM's comfort. It was hard to tell whether he was genuinely happy or just being slick. Either way, BM stayed on guard. Ain't no way in hell he'd let a nigga catch him slipping.

A nigga would have to wake up early in the morning to pull a backdoor move on him. After all, BM *was* the backdoor king.

Lesson 3.16
Take Flight

"Hey, excuse me, miss." Keem called to the flight attendant. Once she approached, he requested two bottles of tequila.

"Coming right up, sir," the woman replied with polite hospitality.

"You good, Boss?" Mia asked from the seat right beside Keem. "I know you got a lot on your mind right now, but you should really try to relax and enjoy this trip. It's been a while since we had a vacation."

"I just feel like I really need to be there with the team. I mean, I know they gon' get the job done and all, but you know I'm used to being on the frontline when shit gets this big. Coming for my team is one thing. Ion play that shit about none of y'all. But coming for my family brings out a whole different monster in a nigga." Keem was so wrapped up in his mind that he hardly noticed the flight attendant return with his drinks.

"Here you go, sir. Enjoy." She laid the bottles on the pull-out table over Keem's lap.

"Thank you. I appreciate your service." With a bright smile she replied, "The pleasure is all mine," before walking away with a light, sassy swag in her hips.

Mia caught the flirtation from the flight attendant while it flew right over Keem's head. She ignored it the same as he did and continued the conversation.

"Trust me, I know how you feel. I was mad as a bitch when you told me I was coming along on this trip. For real, a bitch wanted to be in that field with the gang. Shidd, them pussy-ass niggas took shots at my head too. But then I leveled my head out and thought, fuck it, Las Vegas here we come." The end of her sentence had a hint of humor, but she quickly grew serious again when she noticed Keem's mood hadn't changed. "Naw, for real though, I figured the best place for me is right here by your side. Making sure you win the battle within yourself is my biggest priority right now."

Looking out at the clouds, a thought ran through Mia's mind about what she would do if Keem lost it and went off the deep end. She knew how much the team needed him. And besides all that, she knew how much she really cared about him, whether he knew it or not.

"I'm gonna be alright. We're good. I just need them niggas to wipe the slate clean tonight and get the job done so we can get back to this mission and I can guarantee my baby brother is safe." Mia nodded, believing every word Keem had just uttered.

***

That same night, a little after nine o'clock while Keem and Mia were soaring through the air in the mist of the sun's rays, some of the main members from OGS were slowly rolling through the streets of Petersburg, Virginia, 5th Ward area. "At this point, Ion gives a fuck who I see out this bitch. I'm dead ass bout to start upping on any and every motherfucking thing out this raggedy-ass shit." Simon was heated, yet calm. The anger in his temperament along with the wisdom from his experience provided the balance he needed to be alert on the mission and also thirsty enough for blood to strike like a lion on the hunt.

"This shit's written in stone, my nigga. You can bet your last dollar we ain't leaving this city without some bodies on these throwaways." Simon, the driver, replied to his day one who was sitting right next to him in the passenger seat as he usually did. He went by the name Blick, and it was moments like this that had stamped his name on the streets. Back in his young nigga days, this was the only thing he could push himself to live for. But that was before calming himself down enough to be the main driver for OGS. He wasn't necessarily the best hustler on the team, but a constant one, nevertheless. Always on time, and the money was always accurate down to the single penny. Over the years he had learned to become one hell of a driver. Still though, none of the other traits could replace the fame of his name, Blick.

"Oh, I already know that shit. Ion give a fuck if I have to carve that shit in the cement myself." Blick and Simon had been locked in since day one, even before linking up with Keem. It actually was the uniting of the trio that formed the bond and official establishment of OGS well into their teenage years. "Mane, say less. Nigga already know the vibes right now," to say the two of them took the recent murderous attempts on OGS personnel personally would be a major understatement. "I know one thing, when the time comes for us to get the fuck up out of here—" Simon's words were cut off in the middle of his sentence.

"Come on fool, you know what the fuck going on. That's why I'm the one driving and not you." One argument that would complicate things was which of the two took the attempts the most personally. With the added factors of Shy getting hospitalized from the car crash, the audacity of these niggas bringing that level of disrespect to OGS's front door, and last but far from least, bullets zooming by their own heads whistling threats of death, tensions were high.

"Naw, my nigga," Simon respectfully disagreed. "Yo ass only driving because I need all hands-on deck when it comes to this Drac. You know I swing this bitch like a monkey on a stick." Blick didn't take the comment the wrong way. He knew exactly what Simon was capable of. He also knew that Simon knew the same as him. "I know one thing, yo monkey ass better walk it how you talk it, fool." Still, he talked a little shit knowing it would only amplify the murderous thoughts his longtime partner in crime had flowing through his mind. "Nigga stop fucking playing with—"

"Ayee, y'all niggas see that? Slow down. Slow the fuck down, nigga!" Just as they were passing Indiana Lane, one of the two passengers in the back seat who went by the name Face spoke up, pointing out something he thought worth breaking his concentrated silence over. "Them four niggas that just hopped in that white whip. Get behind them." It was a small group of men deep enough to pack a 2018 Honda Accord. They were walking out of a small yellow convenience store before stepping into the parking lot and climbing into the vehicle.

"Oh yeah, opps on deck! Spot 'em, I got 'em!" the driver said as he swiftly and subtly turned the wheel in the direction of his newfound opps. As expected, they went the opposite way, making it easy for OGS to follow far enough not to be noticed. After a few minutes of riding through the small city, the car pulled up to a very small section of apartment buildings.

"Pull over somewhere right here," Blick suggested. "This motherfucker so small, they ain't got too many places to go," he said, referring to the housing area.

"Dead ass though," Face agreed from the back seat. "The fuck is this? I know this ain't they hood." The question was more of a statement, but his gang caught the drift.

"Nigga, don't tell me you ain't never been out here before?" Simon challenged Face to say what everyone was already thinking.

"Shidd, I ain't ever had a reason to come out this dusty-ass piece of shit," Face replied.

"Them niggas getting out the car," Switch said, changing the subject. He'd been eyeing the car the entire time, waiting for one of them to make a move. "Look at this nigga. Goofy niggas look broke as a bitch. I'd be damned if I die by a broke nigga hand." Once again, Switch had everyone's full attention on the mission.

"Hell, what are we waitin' for?" Face asked, rubbing his finger along the trigger trying to soothe the itch, anxious to apply pressure.

"Hell naw, what the fuck," Switch mumbled to himself under his breath with his hand over his mouth. "I know I ain't fucking trippin'." And he wasn't. The guy who stepped out of the car, who looked like he was on a phone call, was actually sporting a 5th Ward chain that dangled around his neck.

"I'll be damned," Switch said louder this time. His words thickened the tension, and his actions set off a chain reaction that would soon turn deadly.

Swiftly Switch swung open the door and stepped to the perfect firing position. "So y'all niggas think y'all fucking with us, huh?" Upping the pole in his hand, he took aim at the same man he had been watching for the past few minutes. Immediately shell casings ejected as the gun erupted. It was as if the sound of a firearm going off were an alarm, because on cue the rest of OGS spilled out of the car. As promised, Blick clutched the Drac to prepare to take aim. Within the next half second, shots were flying out of the Drac like birds heading south. Blick was excited. He'd much rather set foot on the ground than have to shoot out of a moving car or hop out immediately after the car stopped. Even though he loved the chase of hunting down his prey, it got no better than plucking sitting ducks. Simon was relieved. Being able to take his hands off the wheel allowed him to wrap his palms around his hammers. In his right was a Black Tiger Stripe Magnum Desert Eagle .50 Cal. In the other was a Glock 19 with an extended clip, a beam under the barrel, and a scope on top. Being a little more traditional and nostalgic, Simon preferred a one-shot-to-the-head, two-to-the-chest method. He couldn't wrap his head around firing a hundred bullets at one body, especially if it was the wrong body. Face, always trigger-happy, couldn't wait to scratch that itch. Rapidly he squeezed the trigger, spraying bullets in the direction of anyone who did not pull up with him.

The opps were so caught off guard they didn't know what had just hit them. After retaliating against a considerably powerful organization, you would think they would at least be on ten toes. Who's to say it would have mattered anyway considering the way they were ambushed. At the first sound of gunfire, the man who stepped out of the car along with the few people already standing outside the apartment complex all took off running in their own directions. It didn't help much. Two people out of the bunch were struck down only a few seconds later. The only thing was that neither of them were the man Switch aimed for. It wasn't all on him. Usually, Switch is a great aimer. However, this target made it slightly difficult for a bullet to touch his body. He dipped and dodged, weaving through the slim crowd, ducked behind parked cars, and even used the few buildings that stood amid them. It pissed Switch off so much he thought it was time to live up to his name. Hitting the switches resting on the back of both of his Glocks, he was about to show them exactly why they called him Switch. To make matters even worse, attached to his Glocks were two extended drum clips, giving him enough shots to shoot until God calls him home. Lowering the weapon in his left hand to give his arm a rest, Switch placed all his focus on the aim of the tool in his right hand, even canceling the vision in his left eye to prepare to smack his target.

No matter the distance he put between himself and Switch, the opp that Switch mostly aimed for kept an eye on his predator. Still running for his life, he glanced back. Immediately he noticed the psychopathic look on Switch's face and grew even more terrified. It didn't take a rocket scientist to know what was coming next. The man ducked as low as he possibly could, dodging left behind a stumbling woman. Using both hands, he pushed her aside to make a clean getaway by going around her. That caused the woman to catch a bullet to the head, one to the neck, two entering her shoulder blade, and a handful more barely missing her as her lifeless body hit the ground.

"Fuck!" Switch was pissed at the sight. He lowered both guns this time and took off running after his prey, who was now rounding the corner of a nearby building. Switch shifted gears, picking up speed, trying to catch up before the target got away. He reached the corner in no time, anxious to make this nigga pay for the chase.

"Oh shit! Motherfucker!!" To his surprise, Switch was met with a direct threat to his life. Bullets soared past his head, damn near knocking his brains out of his skull. The first thought through Switch's head was to save his life. Instantly he juked backwards, spinning at a ninety-degree angle and landing his back against the wall.

"This motherfucker done lost his wants-to-live. Nigga can't want to live and keep shooting at me like this."

With his back to the wall around the corner, Switch took a moment to check out the murder scene his team had just put down. The several bodies lying around was what stood out the most. Three were dead for sure. One desperately crawled, striving to get away by any means necessary. Switch suspected the woman was only playing dead, so he decided to let her ride for a couple of reasons he felt were personal.

Bullets chipped the corner of the wall where Switch stood, breaking him out of his sympathetic thoughts. He placed all his focus back on the man trying to take his life. Without hesitating, Switch started throwing bullets back around the corner like the two were playing face-to-face ping pong. Killing this nigga was not getting any easier. The next thing Switch heard were clicks coming from his pistol.

"Fuck!" he cursed himself for not keeping better count of the shells. Returning to the safest position, he pressed his back against the wall. While shielding his body, Switch played it smart and waited for his opp to run out of shots too.

The opp did a good job managing his remaining bullets. It didn't take long for him to realize Switch must have run out as well, judged by the sudden cease of gunfire. The opp thought he had a bright idea: creep up toward Switch so he could stick his head around the corner and catch him unaware. But Switch noticed. The opp hesitated while lifting his gun. Switch jumped back into position and predicted a parade of bullets. Thankfully and strangely, they never arrived. Feeling comfortable, the opp stepped with more purpose and confidence. Soon he realized he'd fucked up worse than he thought. Switch had been cleverer than the opp had given him credit for. When Switch had concentrated on his aim earlier, he'd used only one firearm. If his shot-count calculations were right, the opp still had just enough shots left to set him back a couple steps. As the opp closed the distance, Switch timed his move. Sliding the empty pistol into his waistband, he swapped it for the other in his right hand.

Boc! Boc! Boc! Click! Click! Click! Click!

Switch swung around the corner, determined to knock the face off his opposer. The first shot hit slim in the shoulder, jerking his body back with a snap. He stumbled, taking a few shuffling steps back—exactly what Switch wanted. Those same involuntary movements helped him dodge the next rounds. The first miss flew past his head like a buzzing June bug barely grazing his jawline. The second miss was so far off it was untraceable.

Switch's original intention was to end this by poking holes in his enemy's face. The sound of the clicking gun snapped him out of that deadly daydream. He saw his opponent desperately clutching his shoulder and knew he had to exploit the open wound to survive. Pulling his pants up around his waist, Switch put a little pep in his step and charged. The first two swings were powerful connecting blows—one to the face opened the man up, leaving his ribs exposed to receive the next punch. The opp's body folded as he stumbled back. Switch went to throw another blow but was blocked by the man's forearm. Unexpectedly, the opp countered with a swinging fist that struck Switch just below the temple. From there they traded blows for a few long seconds, until Switch dug his fingers deep into the hole he'd created in the man's shoulder. The pain forced the opp to his knees. Switch wrapped his other hand around the opp's throat and squeezed, not choking all the way but enough to control him.

"Yeah, you bitch-ass nigga. I got yo ass now. That's right, get your bitch ass on the motherfucking ground!"

After the exchange of gunfire and the chaos that erupted in the apartment complex, the OGS team regrouped, assessing the situation and focusing on Switch, who was still covering the vision of their adversary. Simon, frustrated by the delay, called out to Switch, urging him to finish the job so they could leave the area.

Switch, meanwhile, stayed locked in on the immediate threat, talking to himself in the third person and refusing to be distracted by the rest of the crew approaching. Simon grew increasingly agitated, making it clear that lingering wasn't an option, while Blick backed him up, encouraging Switch to handle the situation quickly—or let someone else step in.

Face, never one to hesitate, offered to take over if necessary, but Switch declined, determined to finish what he started—even admitting their target was making it difficult. Still, now he had exactly what he wanted.

"Go get the car!" Switch demanded, expecting no pushback.

"What?" Simon asked, confused.

"Nigga, go get the fucking car! Or do I have to do that myself too?" Switch threw in sarcasm at the end of his command.

"Man, fuck this…" Blick muttered, tired of hearing the back and forth. He marched off toward the car.

"Now get your bitch ass up! Hurry the fuck up!" Switch barked, yanking the man to his feet. He immediately forced him toward the curb a few shoves at a time.

On cue, Blick pulled up with the whip, hopping out to head for the passenger side. Simon took control of the wheel while Switch and Face pushed the kidnap victim into the back seat with them.

"Now can you please explain to me why the fuck we got this opp-ass nigga riding in the car with us?" Blick tried to figure out what the hell they were up to.

"So, you mean to tell me I'm the only one curious enough to figure out what's really going on?" Switch hit them all with something to think about.

"Huh?" Simon frowned, missing the point. "The fuck is you talking about?"

"My nigga, think about it. Do the math, then let me know if the shit adds up to you." Switch didn't hesitate to give the gang a piece of his mind. "Now, I know I play the cut a lot and it might seem like I don't know what the fuck going on, but from the beginning this shit ain't been making too much sense.

"First of all, you got this nigga Ace disappearing up in smoke—into thin air—like his ass never existed. We all seen him that night at the club. Shit, the nigga came with us. Even though Ace was tricking worse than most, he always put us on game whenever he was dipping out the club. Even if it was with a bitch.

"And who was missing all the way up until right before New Year's midnight?" Switch paused, giving it a few seconds to sink in. When he caught the pondering looks on his crew's faces, he smirked. "Exactly. If you know, you know. And who did he walk in with? Right—P."

"What the fuck does all that have to do with this?" Blick pressed, his mind spinning to make sense of it all.

"'Cause nigga, per my calculations, Ace wasn't seen bringing in the New Year at all. Don't let that go over. And not too long after that, not only did P end up dead, but his sister Roxy too. Who was fucking Roxy? Where's P and Roxy from? The people got murdered right in their own living room. That type of shit got a Richmond nigga's name all over it.

"And now all of a sudden, we got smoke with these niggas. For what? You're telling me they just so gangster and bored they had to come fuck with us, huh?"

"And you really think bro was behind all that and none of us knew nothing about it?" Blick asked reasonably.

"Now, that I can't say for sure. All I know is—if it looks like a fucking duck, then guess what? But to answer your question, that's exactly why this bitch-ass nigga is here—to give me the answers I don't know."

At that moment, Switch had the opp by the neck with his pistol pressed to the side of his head. Turning his attention to the man he'd been planning to hurt, Switch made sure he heard him clearly:

"Now, since you out here really willing to die about this shit, please let us know exactly what the fuck y'all niggas problem with us is. Why the fuck y'all pulled up on us at the club that night? What the fuck you got to do with it? And who the fuck was that nigga that showed up at the hospital? The shit better make sense—or I'ma blow your fucking brains all over these back seats."

The ride went quiet. Everyone waited for an answer. The opp shivered under pressure. Face stared holes through him, not blinking once. The last thing the man wanted was to make them more impatient.

"Look, man…" he began, his voice trembling. "I don't know too much of nothing, but—"

Switch tightened his grip around the man's neck, cutting his air off. "Wrong answer, motherfucker!" He rubbed the tip of the gun against the man's face, damn near poking his eye out.

"Wait, brah! Goddamn! You ain't even give me a chance to finish!" The opp froze, waiting for permission to keep talking. Switch caught the signal in silence and gave a single nod.

"All I know is one of our homeboys was supposed to see that nigga Keem walking out the front door of P and Roxy's crib. For a while, it was just a rumor. But brah insisted on proving his point. He got a couple other niggas to believe him, and they started investigating deeper.

"Time goes on or whatever. I'm doing me but keeping my ears to the streets. Word started spreading about how Roxy and P supposedly knew Keem smoked one of his homeboys—or somebody close to him or something."

The fellas looked around at each other but stayed silent as the opp continued to spill his story.

"And for that, Keem was supposed to silence them both. Forensics say Roxy was strangled before she got shot. The story goes that Keem had her on the couch, choking the shit out her. The untouched fast food spilled on the floor near the door showed that P must've walked in and caught him in the act. Like any nigga would, he rushed to help his sister. There was a struggle, and then P's blood was all over the floor.

"Once niggas thought they put it all together, the energy started building about sliding and getting back. The bitches were boosting the most, saying shit like, 'Y'all niggas better get back,' and 'I know y'all ain't gon' let them niggas get away with that shit.'

"Me, I'm just a nigga out here trying to survive. Big dawg out this bitch ended up putting a ticket on dude's head—and I wanted a piece of it. When the first mission failed, another ticket went up for anybody close to the nigga. Now, I'm sure after this, the nigga gon' send the whole city across that bridge."

Looks went around the car that said more than words could. The gang could feel they were in way deeper than they realized—caught up in something they had no clue about.

And on top of all that, who the fuck was this Keem they kept hearing about?

A quiet thought crept into Simon's mind—back to the situation with Mo. Could Keem really have it in him to keep something like this from him? If so, what else was he hiding from his so-called right-hand man?

"Pull over, Stick." It was all Switch could muster to say. For some reason, he felt betrayed. The feeling hit harder than any kill.

The car slowed to a stop. Switch opened the door and stepped out.

"Get the fuck out, nigga. You free to go."

The hostage slowly crawled out of the back seat.

"Oh yeah," Switch added once the man was clear of the car. "It's gon' take your whole city to fuck with us."

A single, deafening thud followed his words. It was the last bullet in his Glock, placed perfectly in the middle of the man's head. The body tumbled out of the car like it tripped over a step and hit the ground hard.

"Get the fuck out my way," Switch muttered, tugging the corpse fully clear so he could get back in.

"Let's go, fool," he said, signaling Simon to drive off.

"So, which one of us up to taking this bullshit to the bossman?" Switch asked, sarcasm dripping from his tone, but honesty was still sharp.

No one had an answer. But in the back of his mind, Simon had questions of his own—ones he planned to address to his longtime friend and now business partner.

Lesson 3.17
Pay the Cost to be the Boss!

It's been a little over three months since E has been home now. Before he was even able to place his feet on the concrete, E already had constructed a plan from the ground up. He even took it a step further and decided to write out his own business plan that was actually accepted within the first thirty days of him putting it in. That helped him get his non-profit organization off the ground fast in a hurry. One of the main things E wanted to do once he was finally free was reach back and help out the younger children in his city. After going through what he went through with his best friend, he wanted to find a way to tie the city even closer together, hoping to build an unbreakable bond for generations on in. On top of that, he was also pushing a pile of boxes of his custom-made T-shirts with his custom-made brand logo. This was just the start of a clothing line that he wanted to breathe life into.

Aside from the legitimate flow of cash, which were only really a passion of E's and bringing in the smaller amounts of cash, he was already damn near knee-deep into the drug game. Unlike BM, E never had the opportunity to test out his hustle, so most of the things he was learning was through hands-on experiences. Not only that, but it was also for the first time as well.

"You got that last O-Z over there with you, right?" E was pulling over the wheels of his GLC 300 Benz alongside the curb of Venable Street near a Virginia ABC liquor store.

"Yeah, I got it. I told you this nigga be flipping fast as a bitch." The passenger handed the sandwich bag full of drugs over to E.

"Damn right! You been on point about most of these niggas. I'm trying to figure out why the fuck I ain't been out here slanging this shit instead of slanging that iron. Shit the same for these bitches too, for real. A nigga been out here slanging this dick up in all of them bitches out here. Nigga got knocked and couldn't get shit. Now I'm only slanging this mother fucker up in one woman. And the crazy thing is, I done got way more out of that one woman than all of them bitches put together. I should have settled down a long time ago. Anyway, you hit brah up and told him we out here, right?" E ended the topic with the focus on the business at hand.

Although he loved the bread, the one thing he hated the most was sitting parked on the curb just waiting for something or anything to go wrong. He still needed some time to get comfortable at this supply and demand exchange. E always kept in mind that he started off as a jack boy himself, so thinking from that perspective always kept him on his toes and just a tad bit nervous.

"Yeah, he hit me back already," the passenger replied. "Nigga coming out now, matter fact."

E unlocked the doors to the vehicle, allowing his customer entrance.

"Sup, fellows?" he asked as he climbed into the backseat of the car and closed the door behind him. E had his eyes locked into the rearview mirror the whole time.

"Man, this mother fucking ride sweet as a bitch, brah!" The two in front lightly chuckled — not too much at the admiration but mainly because he says that every time he hops into the car.

"What I'm trying to figure out is how the fuck do you be moving this shit while your ass be at work like this?" the passenger asked, raising a question.

"Brah, I'm telling you; shit be jumping up this bitch. Shidd, especially when I go on break. Shidd... I had gotten over a quarter off just in those thirty minutes. I sit my ass right on the side of the store, chill, smoke a few cigs, a blunt, and finesse."

E and the passenger started to trip even harder this time, with the man in the back seat joining in with them.

"Shidd, it ain't nothing but them and the winos out this bitch anyway," the man chimed in.

"I don't blame you, my nigga. Actually, I commend you for having the mind to think that up as well as the nuts to pull the shit off," E said while laying the sack in the middle of the armrest. The man grabbed it, replacing it with a stack of cash.

"Already, shidd, same routine. I'ma hit you when I'm done with this mother fucker." He dapped the two up and exited the vehicle. E pulled off and was back into traffic heading to the next destination.

"Shidd, for real though cuz, I'm glad your ass is home, fool. This is the way we always wanted this shit to go for real. Niggas running this bread up together, shinning out this bitch. Plus, we're doing this shit the right way. You feel me? Ain't gotta worry about all that dumb ass beefing with niggas and definitely ain't worried about beefing with niggas in your own gang. I mean, even with the little beef we do have, we're handling that shit like real bosses. You feel me? I mean to the point that niggas don't even know what the fuck is going on."

E knew that everything his little cousin had just said was right. Still, there was that silent doubt in the back of his mind. About if Tru deeply felt what he was saying or was he saying only what he thought E wanted to hear. Either way it went, E knew for damn sure that time would tell it all. And that no matter which way things unfolded, he'd be prepared for either outcome.

"Yeah, I feel you cuz. All niggas gotta do is stay focused and keep it G with niggas. Make sure we stack this paper and keep these businesses up, we're good."

E also knew better than to say too much. In fact, anytime he didn't want to talk about a certain topic, he loved the fact that there were always some businesses at hand to discuss.

"We're ready to head round the south now, right?" E asked a question that he already knew the answer to.

"Hell yeah, go holla at this nigga. This is the last stop for real until later on or somebody hit us early. I already know if it ain't about three or more, then your ass ain't moving." Tru, feeling the tension, aimed to ease it some by throwing in a light joke with the truth.

"Hell naw, nigga, you already know me. Especially when a nigga be wrapped up in some other shit already," E said.

"Shit, it seems like we always wrapped up in something. Niggas in motion like a mother fucker."

Honestly, E couldn't say that he wasn't happy that his cousin Tru made the right decision by siding with him. Even though E was sure that he'd be able to figure it all out on his own, he was grateful to have the people in his corner that he did. And Tru was one of them people.

For starters, Tru was the reason for the speedy overturn of the amount of work that has been flipping. Tru thought it was best to put E on to some of BM's plays. But not just any or all of his plays, but the ones that BM would refer to as "the small plays," the ones that BM would barely miss — a couple of thousand here, a few thousand there. The same plays that would help E get off his amount of work faster while also helping him build his clientele, which led to something else within itself.

E's and BM's work had one main thing in common, and that was that it all came from the exact same place. The one main difference was who the work went to. E's product was leaning more towards the raw side. On the other end, it was hard to tell what BM was stepping on harder, the streets or his work. That question was the reason those same customers that dealt with BM and the product that came with him then turned around and had the opportunity to deal with E — it was a pleasant surprise, like the neighborhood hero coming through and saving the day.

Dealing with E, the streets were able to receive more quality and better quality. The chain reaction only had grown better because now a word was buzzing on the wire that E was the best choice if you were on a certain level. Not to mention, on top of that, E had the nerve to offer his better work at a lower price. Cliché.

Actually, this wasn't a plan of E's. The only numbers he had focused on was the small profit he would make if only he could get the work off within a certain time frame. See, E's main intention was to get Brick his money back as quickly as he could. Some so happen, the method he used came with a positive hit to his clientele. Not to mention the fact that he didn't have to be pressed for money due to the fact that he was already strapped off the strips.

Needless to say, the first three months for E was going great — even greater than he had even imagined. He felt connected to something inside himself that he'd been trying to tap into all his years. Every business he'd built a foundation under seemed to jump off the ground with golden potential.

In addition to the cash flow that Flex was still bringing in from down the jail, which at times came in so fast that E wouldn't even have the time to count it all and would be forced to leave the task to Taira. Speaking of her, it's really been a dream come true. She used her power to help E transform into a whole new man.

E was so deep into his bag that he didn't even feel a need to brag about it. Not a pussy, just a conscious thinker. To E, the come-up was scary. It seemed overnight or more like a setup to him. Like something was just begging him to make the wrong move, so he could get robbed, shot again, betrayed, or locked behind bars.

Even his business with Brick seemed too damn perfect — the way he met, with just a word, the ease that came with moving the work. It was like the more that left, the more there was to return. And then there were suspicions of what BM really might know.

This nigga could pop up any minute, E always thought in the back of his mind as his eyes went back and forth from the rearview mirror back to the street.

***

E and his team weren't the only ones taking off fast. Over the past few months, Derek and Shawndra were already working on selling their third house. The profit from those sales gave them room to move with more speed and confidence. About a month ago, Derek decided to take an eight-week online course to get his real estate license. He only had a few weeks left to finish, and once he did, he'd be able to run that line of business on his own.

But until then, Mark Warner, who was Derek's current agent, loved the business his new, ambitious customer was bringing in. At first, Mr. Warner viewed Derek as a regular man just trying to buy a home for his family's future. Once Derek came back the second time — and as fast as he did — Mark knew then that Derek was on the same mission he himself had been on at the beginning of his own career.

The money was coming in so much faster than usual that it was hard for Shawndra to notice how much Derek was putting away toward a house of their own. He was ready to pop the question, and now their dream home was beginning to take shape in his imagination. He figured, *why not?* This woman had done it all for him up until this point — even things he'd been clueless about.

You'd think that after all the hell Derek went through with his ex, he'd have the sense to run from another relationship. But the fact that he escaped from a demon only to fall into the arms of an angel was, heaven sent. Derek had a feeling he couldn't fully explain when it came to Shawndra. Her energy was pure, her love nonrefundable. She'd go above and beyond for any loyal soul — and even further for the one by her side. There was no one like her. At least, Derek had never met them.

Shawndra was a sweetheart by anyone's measures, but Derek wasn't stupid. Knowing she had a soft spot for him and would do anything for him also meant that if he ever crossed her, there'd be hell to pay all over again. With that in mind, and the love he had for her, he figured — what the hell? He was still from the streets at the end of the day, and he knew one when he saw one. Shawndra was not to be fucked with. *Gangster. Straight rider.*

"Boo, where the hell are we going?" Shawndra asked Derek as she fixed her makeup in the mirror.

"You're about to see now," Derek replied simply.

He pulled over to an empty lot and parked the car.

"Come on, let's see," he said.

Derek's demeanor was calm on the outside, but his chest was pounding like a drum. To say he was nervous would be an understatement.

"Are you serious?" Shawndra asked in surprise. "Your ass is always up to some shit."

When Derek asked her to get dressed and step out with him, she hadn't expected to end up at a dirt lot. But there was one thing that caught her attention — Derek was already walking toward it.

"I know you did not—" Shawndra started to say but stopped herself mid-sentence.

"Shawndra," Derek said as he began to pull the *For Sale* sign out of the ground. He carried it over, placed it at her feet, and got down on one knee. Pulling a little black box from his pocket, he opened it.

"Oh my God!" Shawndra's voice dropped low, filled with disbelief.

"Will you please marry me? I want to be with you for the rest of our lives," Derek said, holding up the ring.

A tear slid down Shawndra's left cheek. "I've never met a person that made me feel this way before. No one has ever loved me the way you—"

"Yes!" Shawndra screamed, her disbelief turning to pure joy. "Yes, I will marry you, Derek! Oh my God, I can't believe this!"

She was nearly at a loss for words as Derek slid the gorgeous ring on her finger. It wasn't the biggest, if she had to admit — but it was pure, and anyone with a blind eye could see it was real. That meant more to her than anything.

Derek rose to his feet and planted the biggest kiss ever on her lips.

"Now, allow me to explain this," Derek said, stepping back to let her take in the view.

"Please do," she replied, matching his polite tone.

"It's ours," Derek said simply.

"What?" was all Shawndra could manage.

"Yup. In a few days we'll be breaking ground to start construction — building our own house, however we want it." Derek's voice carried a new kind of pride.

"I don't even know what to say. I'm just so happy. And all of this... is really real?" Shawndra asked, waving her arms as if to embrace the moment.

"Yup," Derek confirmed again. "And it's all yours."

"It's ours," Shawndra corrected, smiling.

"Right — ours," Derek agreed.

"I love you, and I'm so happy I met you," Shawndra said, her smile shining as bright as the sun.

Lesson 3.18
Losses are life's Lessons

"Any of y'all niggas seen that bitch-ass nigga Tru today?" BM was leaning against his brand-new white-on-white 2025 BMW 330i xDrive, wrapping a gram of weed in a Loose Leaf. The last time BM recalled seeing Tru was sometime yesterday evening. Tru came by, dropped some bread off, re-upped on some more work, and was gone just as fast as he came. BM didn't mind much; he was starting to hate having the little nigga around. It wasn't a soul on earth that BM trusted, but to him, it was just something about having a nigga around that you just know is out to fuck you over. BM had next to little proof of this, but he wasn't dumb. He practically wrote the book on the back-door part of the game. Excluding the fact that Tru has been missing a little here and there, BM expected Tru to spend some time with his cousin—especially knowing how close they were together. The question in BM's head was, would Tru play neutral or use the silent beef between E and himself as a tool for advancement in the ranks?

"Nigga talking about he been laid up with this little bitch or something." With the door wide open, Lil One sat in the driver's seat of a vehicle of his own, phone in hand, scrolling through social media. "I ain't seen the bitch. You know the nigga don't get no hoes. His ass wailing like a motherfucker." Through the eyes of BM, Lil One was another sight to see. Playing his role to a tee, he'd been up on game and present more than most. Lil One grew smarter as the days passed by in his mission. In the beginning, it was difficult for him to be around much. As time went on, he realized just how good he had it. Not to say that he betrayed his original purpose—he was just smart enough to realize that he'd formed another one.

A part of Lil One playing his role was him getting to the bag—something he was doing now like never before. So of course, he figured what the hell; he re-directed his mission, only delaying and not aborting plan A. As time went on, his bag grew bigger and bigger. With that, Lil One may agree that he'd become more comfortable than expected, due to the fact that he had a blindfold wrapped around BM's eyes. Lil One took betraying a wolf in sheep's clothing too far. And here BM was, focusing his attention on Tru, thinking that the cross would come from that way. Can't say he didn't have a reason to expect it too—he should. But never in a hundred years would he think that once the back door flew open, it would be Lil One standing there with the smoking gun. Granted, out of all the main newest niggas, Lil One was all around literally the one. Still, BM hadn't known him long enough to trust Lil One any more than he trusted any of the other Young Niggas Turnt. Funny thing was that BM considered himself the biggest snake. Guess life will reveal reality one day.

One could say that BM was on a hunt for the truth. Maybe even say that BM had learned a few lessons along the way of his life, especially in these recent times. For one, he learned to brag less about his plans and intentions. He'd much rather have the advantage of the element of surprise. It came to him with a sense of power—the shocked expressions on the faces of his peers whenever something came through that he planned. He also learned to stop putting people down as much. Forget the fact that it does not mix with a person telling his every move, giving them more power to pray on their downfalls. Coming to accept some of his own responsibilities, BM noticed that it was his fault that everybody else was treating him the same way. To make matters worse, he received the same hate and negative energy he gave out by a multiplying magnifying number. Even though that didn't stop BM from being him, one of the main intentions for BM calming down was to rock niggas to sleep for enough wiggle room for his snakelike maneuvers. At least he was learning something, I guess.

"Naw, he be trying to get a little play." BM even took up for the youngin Tru—verbally at least, because in his head, Tru was out with E right now planning his world domination. The fact that E was taking so long was driving BM crazy. He didn't know whether he should strike first or wait to see if E had actually said fuck the get-back and really moved on with his life. "That little nigga be snatching some little baddies too, I ain't gon' lie, dead-ass." As BM set a flame to his filled Loose Leaf, he thought to himself with honesty. He knew E was coming; nowadays though, he just wasn't sure when.

E's been moving like a total ghost as far as BM could tell. After the news of his release from jail, E had been completely off BM's radar—like nothing. BM even understood that Tru would cover up for E from time to time. It burned BM's chest up inside knowing that he was being outsmarted at his own game. If anyone knew what E was capable of—it was BM—because he knew exactly what the nigga could do. BM knew that Tru was smarter than him, calmer, a people's person, a nigga full of potential. Now that BM wasn't there next to E keeping his foot on his neck without E having a single suspicion, E was free to run wild and spread his wings. It confused BM more not knowing what type of mind-frame E was in, because in BM's mind that would decide the main factor.

"I know one thing," Bank spoke up, leaning opposite of BM against Lil One's vehicle, "that nigga may have been ducked off lately, but his ass sure has been bringing that bread in. I'm talking about, more than ever." That was a great point Bank just mentioned. "All I'm saying," that same point was the main reason it was hard for BM to complain about the slight absence of Tru—because where his presence was absent, his currency was certainly present.

"On ten, gang!" Shoota said loud enough for his partners to hear from the driver's seat of BM's car. Lil One looked up from the phone directly to the seat purely out of survival instinct. "These niggas—" slyly, he tossed the phone in the opposite seat behind him and pulled his gun out his pants, laying it in his lap. Him and every nigga around him knew who the occupants of the all-black SUVs were. They all remained silent, only communicating through body language. All eyes were locked onto the movement of the vehicles. To their surprise, their eyes followed the trucks make a left, pulling into the same parking lot that they were sitting in. "These niggas better not be ready to come with some bullshit," BM uttered, speaking amongst his crowd.

Windows tinted past legal restrictions, music loud as can be, snatching all the attention of the block. Maine hopped out fly as an eagle, sporting a Washington Commanders jersey, a pair of wheat Timberlands, and dark-blue True Religion denims. "Got damn, what's up shawty?" Maine asked nonchalantly, dusting himself off for no clear reason. Actually, he was a little disappointed in himself, seeing that he had hardly noticed they were posted there before he hopped out of the SUV. YNT stared in silence, not saying a peep aside from some sighs and a couple suck-teethes.

"Oh, y'all niggas gon' igg a nigga like y'all don't hear me, huh? I don't give a fuck," Maine practically said to himself before walking off. "Clown-ass niggas," one of Maine's cousins mumbled to himself with a chuckle as he followed behind his leader, making sure to keep an eye on the members of the opposition.

Shoota climbed to his feet, getting out of the car. He closed the door and walked around to stand beside BM. "What the fuck them niggas doing right here?" He asked an unknown question. "Nigga, it's a free country," BM had to remind his young Shoota. "Duh, fool, but you know them niggas don't come over here like that. Especially when we out here—we got this shit on lock right here, and they know that."

Shoota had been itching to shoot his gun at these niggas since the last time the two gangs had gotten into a minor shootout. The encounter didn't satisfy Shoota's appetite for murder. "Ion know," BM admitted, "but whatever they were on, it was on some in-and-out shit." BM's last statement was more of a matter-of-fact type one, because Maine and his cousin were heading back down the sidewalk just as fast as they had walked up.

"Niggas acting like they don't hear us, but I can tell that they damn sure can see niggas." Maine low-key loved the attention he received from the hood, especially when it came from YNT. Da Fam were actually a good group of guys. They were the type of guys that came back to the hood to give back, lending a helping hand anytime they could. Not that it was anyone's business, but that's exactly what they had made the stop for. Someone needed a little support financially, and Maine took up the responsibility of helping them out. "Y'all niggas supposed to be out here running shit but don't even take care of the people." Maine was now close enough to his car that he could reach out and touch it. "Y'all niggas'll never get the love I get from the hood—y'all lil niggas ain't real enough."

Lil One looked from Maine over to Shoota, who was about to say, "Gang, I'm sick and tired of hearing this nigga's fucking mouth, gang, on God!" Shoota rose up off the car, slanging his arms from one side to another. Lil One shifted his eyes back over towards Maine and noticed that he was locked in on the movements of Shoota. "Every time you pull up round this bitch and we're out here, you always on some bitching-type shit and shit, nigga! Don't nobody be wanting to hear that shit, nigga!" BM laughed out loud, making sure that everyone was able to hear him. Besides, he really did find humor in the statement, along with the facts.

"And?" Maine simply asked, shrugging his shoulders. He was about to reach for the door handle but stopped to make his point. "Little nigga, the fuck you gon' do about the shit?" Maine paused and stared into the eyes of Shoota. Not a sight of fear in either of the two's glare.

"Shit, not a got damn thing! Niggas know what the fuck it is with me." By this time, the other occupants of the two vehicles were beginning to crawl out and spill around the driver's side of the vehicle where Maine was standing.

Lil One clutched his pistol a little tighter and stood to his feet as if he just knew what was about to go down. "Naw, y'all niggas hold on!" BM said as he made his way towards the front of his car, which was parked towards the sidewalk. Lil One bumped into him on his way as he was heading towards the growing crowd. Now, his gun was hanging in his hand, right by his side, ready to be aimed and squeezed.

"Oh what, y'all little niggas finally think y'all ready for this real ass whipping? You know we'll spank this bitch every day for real. Look at your homeboy, he know." Maine indicated towards BM, who was making a clean escape from the looks of it. "We let y'all ass slide the last time. That little petty ass shit y'all niggas called a shootout." Maine laughed a little before looking over to his guys for approval. Of course, they laughed along with him.

At the time, Lil One was thinking to himself; he figured it'd be better if he went ahead and pulled the trigger first. As soon as he was about to turn up his pole, a voice came from the far-right side of the parking lot.

"Maine, y'all always fucking with them little niggas. Maine, leave them little niggas alone, shawty," Tez called out, counting a handful of cash from a play he'd just caught from the car that was pulling off behind him. "The fuck, keep it a hundred, y'all be on some keep the peace when it comes to niggas in the back of the hill. Y'all niggas don't ever bring that bullshit back there. So, why the fuck a nigga be peeping you all up in these little niggas' business and shit like that?" He just had to know.

"Nigga, if you don't mind your motherfucking business. You don't know what the fuck you be talking about, nigga. These little niggas want to be just like me." Maine bust out laughing to himself again. It didn't take long before the rest of his gang started to laugh out with him. "What you, super save these hoes or something?" Maine waved a pointing finger between YNT and Tez. "What, y'all need this nigga to save y'all hoe-ass niggas or something?" He turned his laughter up some more.

"Oh, the nigga talking shit today," Tez replied as he grew closer to the scene. "Shawty, stop playing like you don't know what time it is with me. Niggas already know how we're giving it up!" Maine's frown turned upside down real fast with his last statement. "Okay!!" Tez stuffed the bills into his pants pocket and pulled his cell phone out of the other one. "Give me a sec," he demanded, placing the phone to his ear right after dialing a number. "Ayee—"

"Fuck what that nigga talking about," Lil One uttered to himself loud enough for the people amongst him to hear. Maine focused his attention on Lil One just in time to catch him leveling the pistol to his eye.

"Oh shit!" Maine shouted out, ducking out of the way for what he just knew was coming next. As expected, three shots came flying out of the barrel of the gun. The first one struck a member of the Fam in the shoulder. "Awwhh," the mark screamed out, ducking and running away, trying to pull out a gun of his own. The other two found their way through the material of the car door.

From there, the chaos erupted. They all separated themselves from the center of the commotion, searching for a place of safety. All except Lil One, who was still standing in his exact same spot. Pistol still held high in the air, he swung it left, looking for the right aim on his moving target. However, Maine wasn't going for that shit. And neither was his Fam. Initially, Maine thought it was best to duck for cover, but that idea died quickly once he felt them hot bullets slicing through the air like they had his name on them, personally. That's when he peeked over the hood of his SUV, ready to let that iron sling.

If it was a shootout that Maine was looking for, then by the looks of it, that's exactly what he was about to get. And it seems as if he was the center of attention.

"Fuck!" Maine yelled out to the top of his lungs to himself. Maine noticed that a few members of YNT made gestures that something was going on to the right of them, but they barely reacted. That made Maine see for himself exactly what it was that was catching their eyes. Taking a few steps to the left before leaning forward a tad bit, and now he could see what was going on. It was only a handful of them, but Maine was wise enough to know that each of the men were strong and experienced enough to each be a total handful themselves.

Maine's Fam was already on the mission of backing down Tez's Mosby Top Boyz. In effect, that caused Da Fam to take their attention off of YNT a little too much. Not sure if the Fam were underestimating the Young Niggas Turnt, but I am pretty sure that they assumed that the Mosby Top Boyz were more of a threat. Either way it went, Maine knew that it was time to turn it up—not only one, but a few notches—if he wanted to get him and his team out of here alive. Niggas were coming for blood, and he knew it.

Maine rushed to the passenger side door, which was already open. Once there, he reached for his assault rifle, pulling it from under the seat before heading back to his position. By this time, Lil One had disappeared from his last position and was now nowhere to be found. All that was seen was the sparks of random gunfire going off, specifying the exact places that his opps were hiding.

After scoping the scene for a very quick second, Maine locked into a target that he wanted to tear a hole into with a few bullets from his rifle. He wasn't completely sure who the person was. All he knew was that it wasn't anyone from Da Fam. He gave the Century Arms Micro Draco with the 7.62 x 39 MM drum attached to it a light lift, tugging it in the fold of his arms, starting to take aim. The intended target was a little too close for Maine's own comfort. The first squeeze of the trigger, erupts the Draco, sending a bullet flying in the direction of whoever it was that thought it was clever to shoot hiding behind a car that was right in front of his opposition.

Not sure whether it was the fastest spot for him to take cover at or not, but whoever the person was seemed perfectly fine with where they were stationed. The strike caught Mr. Anonymous off guard. His first reaction was to grab his neck where the bullet had struck, to stop the rush of gushing blood from pouring out. Really didn't matter much, because before you knew it, Maine was squeezing the trigger again, releasing another bullet, sending it straight to the middle of his opp's head. It tapped his melon and exploded like a nut being crushed in between a cracker.

Immediately, Maine scanned the scene for the closest threat in his faculty. Found one ducking back and forth behind the sliding board, no hesitation detected—four shots were sent in that direction. The little nigga stumbled backward, but Maine wasn't sure whether he was hit or not. He paused for a second to indicate any movement. That led to him watching the little nigga scooting backward, struggling to get to his feet. Maine knew better than to give him that opportunity. A couple more shots were sent to his current target just so he could see what he would do next.

Far from Maine's expectations, the target had the right nerve to roll over on top of the fake maneuvers to avoid any bullets that may come in his direction. Maine thought it was a smart move, but the sight of seeing someone actually do it in real time made him want to burst out in laughter. If the situation wasn't so serious at the moment, he would have.

Instead, he lifted his weapon again, preparing to finish the job.

Before he could even pull the trigger again, a bullet smacked the piece, damn near knocking it clean out his hand. He reached for it, but another round tore straight through the meat of his palm. He gritted his teeth, winced a little, but the moment came and went too fast for anybody to notice. Acting off pure instinct, Maine snatched the handle with his left hand and tucked that bitch tight in the pit of his arm, looking to get it back in blood.

Once the gun was secure enough for his standards, Maine aimed the weapon right where the shots had just traveled from. He only had time enough to catch BM pop out from behind the trash can, throwing three more shots towards his way. On instinct, Maine ducked and rolled around the other end of his car.

On his way to what he thought would be safer than the position that he was already avoiding, the gun had flown out of Maine's hand. It was only a few steps away. But those few steps could cost him his life—especially due to the fact that he was now exposed to a whole different set of opps.

Lesson 3.19
The Price is High

Lil One was aware that as soon as he let off that first shot that all hell was bound to break loose. He couldn't have been any further from the truth. What in the hell did he give an ounce of a fuck for? This wasn't his hood. These weren't his people, his niggas. In fact, he was here for this very purpose, vengeance through murder.

With YNT blowing their horns in each and every direction, between Da Fam returning fire targeting the necks of their younger peers and including the fact that now a few of the Mosby Top Boyz were now involved in this pre-massacre, Lil One thought it'd be best to find some cover. That is if he'd planned on making it off this crime scene. He was able to slide behind the sliding board just in time to see the first bullet chip off a piece of Pickle's neck. He noticed the shock in Pickle's eyes, the desperation he put into grabbing his neck as if it was his last and final purpose on earth. Like, if that didn't work then he knew it'd be over with. It was something about that moment of Lil One watching Pickle struggle for his life that seemed to last forever. It was like a picture that a cruel God was sticking in Lil One's face, forcing him to look at it with his eyelids forced open in a somehow torturous manner. It was something about Lil One soaking in the image with his eyes that poured down into his chest and entered his heart. If it wasn't sympathy, it was similar. It was something in Lil One that made him want to defend this person who he'd only pretended to befriend.

At this point all Lil One could do was beg for this scene to leave his sight. Immediately he regretted the prayer answered because the second bullet was entering Pickle's head, dismantling it as if it had the weight of a bulldozer. Lil One's heartbeat intensified to a rate that he thought was impossible. The fear from the thought of the exact same thing happening to him triggered his fight-or-flight senses. Being that Lil One has been a fighter his entire life, he trained the weapon in the direction of the bullet that had recently stolen the life of Pickle.

It pissed Lil One off when he caught a glimpse of Maine spinning around the other end of the car, making it almost impossible for him to get a good shot. BM ran him off with a few surprising shots of his own. From Lil One's perspective, Maine had gotten struck somewhere in the hand. Ironically, Lil One felt the same as BM felt about that tap on the hand—it wasn't enough. Taking the opposite route that BM decided to pursue, Lil One thought it was best for him to sprint through the playground, heading towards the end of Maine's car and cut him off from around the other end, trapping Maine in between BM and himself. Initially it was a good idea. That's if it wasn't a parking lot full of bloodthirsty, trigger-happy gunslingers running around faster than an Olympic track tryout, ducking and dodging like they were in a boxing ring instead of punching— throwing bullets with high hopes of knocking someone's head off. That someone was Lil One.

As soon as he took his first step off the playground's surface a bullet was soaring past his head too fast for his eyes to catch. But the whistling sound flowing through the wind was undeniable. "Oh shit! Bitch," Lil One uttered to himself, changing the direction of his attention. Way towards his left he spotted a member from Da Fam preparing to send another shot his way. Too bad for him that he didn't spot BM crouched in between a couple vehicles waiting for a perfect opportunity to pounce on his prey. And that's exactly what he did. BM shot twice, but it only took one bullet to send the target's body collapsing to the ground.

"Take cover, nigga!" BM shouted towards Lil One right before ducking back down into his hiding spot that was now blown. It was obvious to Lil One that BM hadn't made it to Maine either. In fact, so much was going on that it was fairly easy to forget all about Maine. After taking BM's advice, Lil One reconsidered his approaching role in this warfare. One of the first things he thought about while hiding behind the steel green trash can was that now was the perfect time to snatch his revenge from BM. He had to remind himself that his beef with Maine was just a front. Although he could care less if every one of these niggas wiped each other out to the point of extinction, as long as he was the one that sent BM under, he'd be satisfied.

Lil One took a little peep around the corner of the trash can to get a view of what was going on. Much of the same. BM was nowhere in sight, which caused Lil One to continue his scan of the scene. Silently he saluted Shoota for the performance he was putting on thus far. Shoota was banging the AAC Honey Badger as if he was in the middle of a Call of Duty video game. He took a couple down with acute accuracy. The rest he backed down and pushed back without an issue. Lil One always fucked with Shoota's gangster. It was original. He was not trying to be a follower or out here doing certain shit for the approval of others. In Lil One's eyes, that nigga Shoota was unapologetically himself. Not expected to be too far away from him was Bank. With two guns up, he covered the backside of Shoota, making sure that no one would be able to catch him lacking from the blind side. Aside from Bank's hustle, the thing that stood out to Lil One the most about Bank was his loyalty. Regardless of who, what, when, and where, Bank was always down to back the cause—with his dollars or backing it up with his pistol. The why was never a major concern. Whatever his niggas were with, Bank was certainly down with the flow. On the opposite side of the shootout, Drip was going crazy, aiming to put a bullet into whoever he could reach. Meanwhile Cee wore a face full of tears as he held Pickle in his arms for one last time. His gun was sliding out of his hand, halfway resting on the ground. The sight triggered a tragic moment in Lil One's life that made him snap.

The thought of him not even being able to hold his best friend before he left pissed him off to the point that he was not even sure if he cared about living at this moment. He went deep into his mind and could remember and feel the pain as if it was just yesterday. He could feel the blood soaking through his clothes as if he was floating in a pool of water. The ringing of his ears as the bullets erupted until he was able to hear nothing at all. The aftermath of waking up to the news that someone had attempted to murder you and had succeeded at taking out your soul brother—everything, it all came back rushing like the waters of a newly released dam. All that other shit flew clean out the window. All the money he was getting, the cars, fresh clothes, all the girls, just the ability to brag and say, "nigga, I'm getting money," was no longer something that Lil One could fake as if it was all somehow making him happy and all of a sudden super forgiving. Fuck that, he wanted blood. "I'm about to make this nigga feel it." That was all he said before he snuck off to his next cover spot in pursuit of wherever it may be that BM was ducked off at.

Lesson 3.20
Strike Quick

"What! Shit! Alright, nigga, I'm on my motherfucking way! Say less. Get the fuck off the phone!" Tru threw the phone in his lap and cursed himself one more time.

"Damn, man. Ayee, cuz, take me to the Hill right quick," Tru asked E, who was operating the vehicle at the moment.

"For what, nigga, what the fuck going on up there?" E was purely concerned about what it was that his little was about to run off and get into. He could care less about the nosiness of anyone's business. "Plus, you know I don't even go round that motherfucker at all. I got my own shit going on and I plan to continue moving the way I've been moving. That way I can make sure that shit goes as smooth as I need it to."

Tru agreed. E had a valid point. But he wondered if E would think the same if he was aware of what was going on now on top of that hill. Would he change his plans and try to take advantage of a snake that was already cornered in? It was a good enough question to itch Tru's curiosity. So much so that he just had to know the outcome.

"Ion know, Cuz, this might be your chance right here," Tru simply said as if he expected E to know exactly what he was talking about.

"What? What the fuck is you talking about?" This whole shift of energy was pissing E off. Here he was, on his way to handle a little business before hitting a few stores and picking up some shoes and clothes. A single phone call had the potential to change his whole destiny, especially if he didn't play his hand right. E had every right in his mind to go against Tru's request and continue on with what they already had planned. But now, even E's mind was so scrambled that he demanded answers from Tru himself.

"I keep asking you fucking questions, and all you're coming back with is a bunch of bullshit. Nigga, talk straight and say what the fuck you got to say, so I can know what the fuck I'm getting into before I pull my whip up here and them niggas see my shit. Get my shit exposed and shit. Then I'm really gone have to get into some shit."

E went off for a second, to the point he wouldn't even give Tru a chance to speak, even if he tried to.

"You finished?" The nonchalance of the question from Tru pissed E off even more. If Tru didn't watch it from this point, he might cause E to take his building frustrations out on him soon.

"Nigga, stop fucking playing with me." That was Tru's hint.

"Them niggas up there banging it out right now," Tru spilled out, as if he was talking about a kiddie fight on the playground and not something similar to a war across the seas.

"Who?" was all E could muster to utter.

"Everybody." Tru paused after his simple response. They both took the time to allow the news of what was happening to sink into their brains. It wasn't as long as it seemed before Tru broke down with a few more facts about the situation. "The nigga Pickle from Creighton dead. They got them old-ass Mosby Top Boyz out there getting it in. I think they said Maine got hit and some more."

E was dumbfounded at the words he was hearing. "So, you mean to tell me that it's y'all little YNT niggas, Maine, Da Fam and them, and MTB up there all getting at each other?" he asked, for confirmation.

"Yeah, I know it's a lot. That's why I was gone say you don't even have to take me all the way up the hill. I don't even wanna go up that far anyway. I'ma just creep up from the back."

E heard Tru but overthought his cousin's plan. "You sure?" he asked, wanting to make sure.

"Yeah, hell yeah," Tru assured. "How it's gone look if I don't pull up? Especially after them niggas done called me and everything."

E didn't have to think long before it made sense. Regardless of whether Tru wanted to protect what was supposed to be his gang or not, he still had a role to play. And he was right — it would look betraying if Tru didn't show up in defense of YNT.

"You know what?" E asked, right before answering his own question. "You right."

By the time they were done with their conversation, E was already at the bottom of Mosby. He came up from by the jail and under the bridge, where people would be less likely to see him — especially at a moment like this. E pulled halfway up the hill before making a quick U-turn and parking in front of the bus stop.

"I'ma get up with you," Tru announced as he was removing the rifle from under the seat he sat in. "Make sure you hit me up, fool."

A part of E was already remorseful for dropping his baby cousin off in the middle of a war zone, knowing he wouldn't be there to have his back. On the other hand — the hand that allowed E to carry on with his decision — was a sense of pride. It gave him a little more confidence knowing that Tru was brave enough to stand his ground and hold his own.

"Nigga, say less." Tru rushed out of the car and slammed the door shut. E pulled off slower than he initially wanted to, but Tru gave him reason to go about his day.

Tru sprinted up the hill as fast as he could, toting the rifle in his hands. It took him no time to get halfway up the hill. For some reason, Tru couldn't wait to get to the action. He wasn't sure if it was for the chance to use his brand-new assault rifle that he'd only had the chance to test out, or if it was the opportunity to finally show both of them shit-talking ass niggas — Maine and BM — exactly what he was made of. Tru felt as if they both underestimated him on multiple levels, especially BM when it came to what Tru felt he brought to the table. He figured now was his time to show them both.

The shots could be heard the moment he pulled up. The closer he got to the scene, the louder they grew. Tru sneaked past a bush and crept up to the corner of the building. From there, he scoped out the scene to see what was going on. As well as get an angle on his position. Luckily for him, he had come out on the right end of the cut — landing him right in the corner of YNT. It was such a perfect entrance that no one had even seen him make it, as if he'd been there all along. Considering he was already late to the party; Tru thought it best not to waste any time and get straight to the point. After using his instinctive ability that had developed over the years, he was able to pinpoint the main setup — where his niggas were, where they were sending their shots, and where they were coming from.

The first thing he did, making his presence known, was send a few shots toward an opp that had somehow found a way to creep up on Shoota and Bank. Had it not been for Tru, the intruder might've succeeded at infiltrating one, if not both of them. He didn't hit his target — actually, he wasn't even close. In Tru's defense, the distance was quite far. But the bullets caused enough of a distraction to throw off the opp's focus.

Bank caught the end of Tru standing across the field holding a smoking gun. It made him feel good to know he could count on his nigga Tru like this — especially after the gang was just having a conversation about how much he'd been missing in action lately. The fact that he popped up out of thin air the way he did, in addition to him passing the assist as soon as he touched the field, said a lot.

The assist metaphor fit — the gunfire from Tru made Shoota aware of the invading intruder. Immediately, while he had him slipping in the middle of the field, Shoota took advantage of the opp who had just fucked up by stepping out of bounds. He thought he had caught him a couple sitting ducks, but there was no way he could've planned for one of his main opps popping up out of nowhere and interrupting his plans.

That was the last thing he was able to think about — because the next moment, his body was tumbling to the ground as the life's substance flew into the air. Initially, it only took one shot for Shoota to end the life of the person who'd been seconds away from taking his own. But for some reason, he felt the need to go above and beyond to prove a point, dumping a handful of extra bullets into the torso of the fallen corpse.

More than mad that Maine was able to get away, Tru thought it was best to pop out, getting an up on the vehicles before they were able to pull off fully. On his way to putting himself in the perfect position for firing, Tru spotted BM. For some strange reason, Tru had a quick thought of letting off a few shots at BM. Hell, he felt a small sensation just from the thought of being able to release one shot his way— long as it was the one that laid BM down for good, and that he was able to get away with being the one to let off the shot.

The thought escaped the nerves of his brain the moment he realized that he'd just got caught lacking in the field. It was the shots zooming past his head, kicking up dirt from the ground, that caught his attention. Da Fam were backing out without care as to who may be in the way of the moving vehicles. At the same time, they used that moment to aim out the windows at their targets, hoping to leave most, if not all, of these bastards stretched out over the ground.

With the Mosby Top Boys backing out of the war, it allowed Da Fam more room to make their escape. Maine was in the passenger seat, but Tru could see his face as clear as day. At first, the look on his face disgusted Tru to the point that he wished every bullet he'd sent toward Maine had connected directly to his face. But then something changed—something that puzzled Tru's curiosity. As a matter of fact, it was the same exact expression that Maine now had spread across his face.

Tru wondered what could have happened, what hadn't happened in these last past minutes he'd been on the scene, that was so difficult to digest now. The actions of Da Fam all became suspicious as they suddenly stopped shooting out of the blue, as if they had won the war and it was all over with now. Tru knew that was far from the truth—mainly because he was still standing, and as long as that was a fact, Da Fam would always have a problem on their hands. The looks on their faces expressed otherwise.

Tru was growing more anxious by the millisecond. He started to look around at his surroundings to see if he could notice anything that was too off. It didn't take him long at all to figure out what the problem was.

Lesson 3.21
Time to Pay UP

BM's body buckled to the ground from the bullet that had previously pierced the knee of his leg right above the patella. In the midst of the *trip*, his body remained an open target for a couple more bullets to enter his torso and, finally, the last contacting the area of his head, which seemed to be the deadliest of them all.

The ceasefire from Da Fam was starting to make much more sense. The head of the snake had finally fallen from its body. The king of YNT was down. This battle was done. While a few members of YNT held down the team, making sure that Maine and Da Fam were actually planning to leave the scene and not trying to get any extra shots in, aiming to take another member down, the rest of the members rushed over to BM's side, making a circle around his body. He was silent while everyone waited for him to utter a word for some type of sign.

Tru rushed from his position over to the circle of YNT. "Watch out!" was the first thing he said once reaching his new destination. "He alright?" was the second. Tru squeezed himself through the crowd, fighting to get a clear visual of BM. Before he was able to lay eyes on the fact of it being real or not, Tru was in disbelief. He knew BM wasn't unstoppable and that we all bleed the same, but to see it with your own eyes, having the physical acknowledgement that it had actually happened, was a whole different thing within itself. Another thing to Tru that crossed his mind was who was the person that had gotten the shot off on BM, sticking him to the ground like a crawling caterpillar. To think, Tru was just considering the thought of taking a shot at BM himself. He was surprised at how someone had the same idea as him, along with the balls to do it. And that question amplified: who did it?

Next were Shoota and Bank, running up a little late to the crowd but in a rush, nonetheless. Also, it wasn't as if most of them hadn't just seen the two of them at the edge of the parking lot moments before heading over. They were the main two escorting Da Fam from the apartments sitting on the top of Mosby Court Projects, so it was easier to excuse their tardiness with them and the few other members marching right behind them. Watching as they gathered all together, YNT were deep. The crazy thing about it was that this was the very first time they'd all been together — as in, each member. Well, that was except their newest member and, of course, Pickle, who was still laying over to the side, and Drip, who still held his friend in his arms, still bawling, face full of tears. Drip was just not here mentally or emotionally. Then finally Lil One arrived.

"Who the fuck is that?" he asked, as if he really didn't know. He seemed interested, but it was hard to tell. First of all, where the fuck had he been for the past minute or so? And how was he the only one that didn't know that BM was hit by now? Everyone in the field was on game about that. Even Tru knew who it was before he was able to see. But really, none of that mattered, because somehow Lil One was able to cause a very believable distraction. "That's BM?" was his next question. There was no need for an answer though. "What the fuck?" Because it was now obvious to him. Once he laid eyes on BM lying helpless, a great deal of mixed emotions rushed through his body. Honestly, he didn't know whether he should be happy that BM was knocking on death's door, or if he should be mad. But mad for what though? Was it due to the fact that he had taken a shot at BM and missed? I guess that makes sense. Or was it because someone else had gotten to BM before he could? That could be a valid point as well. Or how about the fact that regardless of who had the privilege of shooting BM, his ass was still lying here in front of Lil One's face fighting for his life.

That's when it hit Lil One. It all came back to him at once. The feeling was like being born as a baby and knowing everything that you already needed to know without having to learn it. In other words, it wasn't good. It was painful, agony — not just physical, but mental and spiritual as well. It was the struggle of death, the process of being eliminated, through an intensity of violence and a broad understanding of the origins of pain. The realization that there is no avoiding struggle or pain without metamorphosing into a higher level of consciousness. Accepting the fact that this is just what it is: you either win through the struggle of growth or die. It was the very same unexplainable waves of energy in motion that Lil One had ever experienced. Therefore, he knew exactly what BM was going through at the moment. The sense of helplessness alone was enough to drive any person insane.

"Damn," he mumbled, although the mumble was purposeless. It really was due to the remembrance of all that BM had put him through. He was reminded that his friend Crow was actually the lucky one. *Just because you make it through the pain doesn't mean that it's necessarily gone. It's always waiting dormant, waiting for something to remind you of its existence, taunting you with the fact that you'll have to live with that pain forever. Yeah, you're a champion because you made it through, but champions are built through pain and are reminded every chance they get that they're nothing without it.*

"Who in the fuck shot my nigga?"

After sitting there taking it all in for a few seconds, Shoota finally snapped out and lost it. He pushed his way through and away from the crowd, removing his pistol from his waist again, waving it into the air and without a lick of hesitation firing off three or four shots. "I swear to fucking God, if niggas don't start fucking talking right now!" Shoota's demand was heard loud and clear. The only thing was that no one said anything because no one knew what to say. They didn't know what to say because they were all asking the same question.

"I wasn't anywhere near this spot," Lil One said in his own defense. "I ain't even know brah was hit. A nigga had to run all the way over here just to see who it was." No one paid too much attention that Lil One was the first to speak up. Was he doing it out of a guilty conscience, or because he was one of the leaders in the bunch and speaking up something he was supposed to do? "The shit crazy as hell, cause brah was just right there with Shoota and me getting down on niggas. Then all of a sudden, I look back and its man down." Bank expressed the confusion from his point of view.

"Naw, dead-ass though," Shoota yelled, still snapping as he made his way back to the crowd. "Brah was just right there with us. And the crazy thing about it is that there wasn't no opps around us for real. As a matter of fact, we was just stepping on them MTB niggas, flushing they asses out. That's how the Fam was able to slide off, because them niggas was blocked in the whole time." With Shoota vouching for the story that Bank had just laid down, that kind of pulled the two out of the lineup of suspects that may have tried to kill BM.

"And I say all that to say, yes, I feel like this was an inside job — like one of y'all niggas that's looking me dead in the fucking face right now just tried to knock the crowd off the nigga that put all of us on our motherfucking feet!" The more Shoota spoke the more it sunk in exactly what was happening, which in return pissed him off even more.

"Yeah, that's some fucked up shit," Lil One verbally agreed. He actually felt as if Shoota wasn't talking to him in some type of way. Lil One, knowing exactly what he had come here to do in the first place, wasn't about to allow none of the shit that Shoota was talking to get to him. Besides, as far as he was concerned, he was standing his ground that he wasn't the one that plugged BM to the concrete even though he desperately wished that he was. So, with that being said, he allowed Shoota to ramp on, even hyping him up some along the way, playing the role to a tee.

"I'm telling niggas now, this shit gone come out, and when it do, a nigga gone have to deal with me. I promise on my mama's life I'ma make that happen." By this time the sirens were blaring from down the street, and everyone knew where they were headed to. Neighbors were beginning to poke their heads and feet back outside the doors, hoping that it was safe enough to step back outside, trying to see what was going on now that all the smoke had cleared.

"Shoota, take my tool and put it up for me," Bank asked. "I'ma stay right here with brah."

Shoota looked confused. "What?" he asked. "Hell naw, nigga. We're getting the fuck out of here. Nigga, it ain't no telling how many cameras we on out here chopping shit down. Shidd, the bossman is already down. I can't lose my right hand too."

The last statement that Shoota responded with made sense enough for Bank to change his mind. "Alright, brah, you right," Bank agreed. Before stepping off though, he kneeled down to get closer to BM. He could tell that BM was still breathing and fighting for his life, but unfortunately, he was unresponsive at the time.

"Listen, big brah," Bank began, knowing that BM was not in the condition to talk, "I know you going through hell of pain right now, but you a fucking soldier, nigga. You don't quit, you fight, nigga. So, fight. Get your shit together so you can get back to the gang. We got way too much unfinished business to be clocking out niggas now. Look at how far you came. Look at how far you brought niggas. You gotta know that this shit ain't over with for you, my nigga. Now fight.

We're going to be down to see you. And while you're down there, we're going to make sure we keep this shit up and running until you're up and ready to take back your throne. Love, fool."

Bank stood to his feet. "Love, fool. Love you, BM. See you later, fool. I'm right behind the ambulance."

Most of the others had stood by, listening to the vow that Bank gave to BM, silently agreeing to take the same oath.

"Y'all niggas, let's roll," Shoota ordered after Bank decided to walk off. "We gotta make sure we put all this shit up. Y'all know they about to smack this bitch."

Without protest, YNT, for the first time in history, was taking orders from a new general. The anxiety of it all was whether it was permanent or just a temporary thing.

The whole YNT walked off together, all besides BM, Pickle, and Drip, who refused to leave his friend's side. On the other side was BM, who may still have a fighting chance, left lying without a soul on his side. Yet, Pickle was definitely a goner and still received one hundred percent loyalty from his friend.

I guess you could say that this is the price that BM paid to be the boss. All the scheming, plotting, betrayal, strategically causing chaos in the lives of others, stepping on any and everybody's toes, just to be lying helplessly and lonely by himself on a ground that seemed to grow colder by the second. Or was it his body that failed to produce the heat needed for his body to survive?

The crowd had moved out the way just in time for the police to come through with the crime scene ribbon, taping most of the section off to the public. Next, BM could hear the ambulance pulling up and paramedics hopping out of the vehicle. All he could do was hear and think to himself, which at this moment felt like the exact same thing to him for some reason.

"Alright, buddy, here we go. You're going to feel a little bit of pain," what sounded to BM like the lead paramedic said. A little pain was a damn lie. Once the team of paramedics lifted BM's body and rolled him onto the carrying stretcher, it felt as if he could feel every pain ever known to man.

This moment was one of the only times that BM had mustered to utter anything close to a word. One thing he knew for sure was that from there, the fight was on. The entire time lying there on the ground, one of BM's main thoughts or hopes was if the paramedics would make it there in time before he laid there and bled out all of his life's source. He knew that if he could remain conscious, breathing, and still able to hear what was going on, he just might have a chance to make it back to his feet.

As soon as the thought of him standing on his feet once again came, it gave BM the sense of power that he always cheated life out of. And he couldn't wait to get that power back into his hands. The first thing he would do was secure his power in a safer way. Following immediately afterward would be him replacing the power in his hands with a firearm of any kind. He didn't give a fuck what type of gun it was at this point, as long as the mother shot the bullets out of the barrel and got the job done. The first person he would aim to kill was the person that had just attempted to take him out. He couldn't wait to see if he would be able to make it through the biggest fight of his life. BM knew from this day that if he just so did make it through, it would be hell to pay.

BM did well with remaining calm up until this point, but now, lying in the back of the ambulance in the center of all the commotion and chaos, BM's heart rate intensified rapidly.

"Okay, try to remain calm," the lead paramedic spoke in an attempting soothing tone, but the alarming concern was still able to be detected by BM. That caused him to grow eagerly curious about the happenings in the outside world. Momentarily, BM's worlds were split between the ins and outs because it was as if he was unable to open his eyes no matter what he did to try.

Concluding the fact that he was lacking the power of control would have driven BM over the wall, only if he could gather the strength to do so. Imagine going crazy as a bat and can't. You can't move, could barely feel, and may be lucky to push a syllable out of your mouth.

"Yeah, we're definitely going to need something to calm this guy down with." A request was made for a type of sedation medication to put BM to sleep. "You have to remain calm, so we'll be able to perform our jobs correctly. Sue, you're going to have to rush it a bit there."

The same person that was throwing out the commands was the same person using his hands, trying to hold BM down by his arms. It scared BM like he'd never been frightened before in his whole entire life. To the point that he was able to build up the strength to pop up on the bed, sitting completely upright, to peel his eyelids apart, allowing him the fair chance to see everything around him again.

It was a good thing that BM wasn't able to see, because as soon as he had the privilege of doing so, he turned panic into a total disaster. Laying his sight on the scene around him did nothing but confirm the only one thing that BM was still uncertain of—and that was if any of this shit was even real.

Is any of this even happening for real, or is it all just one sick-ass bad dream that he was hoping to wake up from anytime now? But nope, it was all so very real. As a matter of fact, shit had gotten too real.

A couple sets of hands aided one another as they forced BM back down to the bed. "Now! Go, I got him!" The same voice gave another demand, waiting for one of his partners to place the needle in BM. A few staggering seconds later, and the team was successful.

It may have seemed much longer to BM, but it took less than a minute before BM's body was sinking into a relaxation of painless bliss. It amazed BM at how fast he could go from feeling the worst pain ever and being presented with the most horrifying fear of his life, to the most wonderful feeling he'd ever had the blessing to imagine.

He wasn't sure whether this was it or not. He sure did hope that the paramedics knew exactly what they were doing and didn't give a shot that may have just sped the process of his death up. Because if he didn't know any better—which, ironically, was the truth—he could have sworn that this feeling was exactly that. It must be. It has to be.

Couldn't tell you just how stupid BM felt in the moment, trying to convince himself that he was certainly dying, even though of course he prayed that wasn't the case.

This was a serious moment of clarity for BM. Honestly, he was a bit disappointed in himself. He didn't feel as if he did too bad for a nigga coming from the bottom with nothing. But it was nowhere near close to having the power of the whole world in his hands.

So, for the first time ever in his young twenty years of living, BM decided to quiet his thoughts and say a prayer to himself. Even he couldn't tell you where it came from, but a deep hope went out that the world had said their last prayers as well. Because if God had chosen to answer BM's prayer, then they'd surely need theirs answered too.

Lock Down Publications and Ca$h Presents
Assisted Publishing Packages

Due to an increase in the price of services we have increased our prices. The prices below reflect the price increase as of 11/1/24.

BASIC PACKAGE	UPGRADED PACKAGE
$699	**$1000**
Editing	Typing
Cover Design	Editing
Formatting	Cover Design
	Formatting
	Upload eBooks to Amazon
	Upload Paperback to Amazon
ADVANCE PACKAGE	**LDP SUPREME PACKAGE**
$1,400	**$1,700**
Typing	Typing
Editing (line editing/content)	Editing (line editing/content)
Cover Design	Cover Design
Formatting	Formatting
Copyright Registration	Copyright Registration
Proofreading	Proofreading
Upload eBooks to Amazon	Set up Amazon Account
Upload Paperback to Amazon	Upload eBooks to Amazon
	Upload Paperback to Amazon
	Advertise on LDP's Amazon and Facebook Page

***

Other services available upon request.
Additional charges may apply

Lock Down Publications
P.O. Box 944
Stockbridge, GA 30281-9998
Phone: 470 303-9761
Email: lockdownpublications@gmail.com

Submission Guideline

Submit the first three chapters of your completed manuscript to ldpsubmissions@gmail.com. In the subject line add **Your Book's Title**. The manuscript must be in a Word Doc file and sent as an attachment. Document should be in Times New Roman, double spaced, and in size 12 font. Also, provide your synopsis and full contact information. If sending multiple submissions, they must each be in a separate email.

Have a story but no way to send it electronically? You can still submit to LDP/Ca$h Presents. Send in the first three chapters, written or typed, of your completed manuscript to:

LDP: Submissions Dept
P.O. Box 944
Stockbridge, GA 30281-9998

DO NOT send original manuscript. Must be a duplicate. Provide your synopsis and a cover letter containing your full contact information.

Thanks for considering LDP and Ca$h Presents.

NEW RELEASES

BLOODLINE OF A SAVAGE 1-3
THESE VICIOUS STREETS 1-3
RELENTLESS GOON 1-3
BY PRINCE A. TAUHID

THE BUTTERFLY MAFIA 1-3
BY FUMIYA PAYNE

A THUG'S STREET PRINCESS 1&2
BY MEESHA

CITY OF SMOKE 3
BY MOLOTTI

GET IT IN SLUGS 1 &2
BY B. STALL

STANDING ON HER BUSINESS 1&2
BY DG SANTANA

STEPPERS 1,2&3
THE REAL BADDIES OF CHI-RAQ
BY KING RIO

THE LANE 1&2
BY KEN-KEN SPENCE

THUG OF SPADES 1&2
LOVE IN THE TRENCHES 2
CORNER BOYS
BY COREY ROBINSON

TIL DEATH 3
BY ARYANNA

CRIME PAYS 3 | SELF MADE TAY

THE BIRTH OF A GANGSTER 4
BY DELMONT PLAYER

PRODUCT OF THE STREETS 1-3
BY DEMOND "MONEY" ANDERSON

NO TIME FOR ERROR
BY KEESE

MONEY HUNGRY DEMONS 1-2
BY TRANAY ADAMS

HUB CITY MENACE 1-3
BY J. WHITE

A THUGGISH PASSION 1&2
LAND OF DA HOOLIGANZ 1-4
KILLAZ ON STANDBY 1&2
BY IRA B.

FO'EVA ROLLIN 1&2
BY ASSA RAYMOND BAKER

THE LEVEL UP 1&3
BY LUXURY KING

Coming Soon from Lock Down Publications/Ca$h Presents

IF YOU CROSS ME ONCE 6
ANGEL V
By Anthony Fields

A THUGS STREET PRINCESS 3
By Meesha

CORNER BOYS 2
By Corey Robinson

THA TAKEOVER
By Keith Chandler

BETRAYAL OF A G 2
By Ray Vinci

SAVAGE FAMILY EMPIRE 1&2
SOULLESS GOON 1,2&3
THE DIRTY SIDE OF MONEY 1,2&3
By Prince

FOR MY ENEMY'S SAKE
AMBITIONS OF A SLIDER
FRESH OFF DA PORCH
By IRA B.

BY THE TRUCKLOAD 1-4
TIPPIN' THE SCALES 1-3
BAD BITCHES WIT GUNZ 3
PROBLEM SOLVED 2
By Christopher "Diesel" Hornezes

Available Now

RESTRAINING ORDER 1 & 2
By **CA$H & Coffee**

LOVE KNOWS NO BOUNDARIES 1-3
By **Coffee**

RAISED AS A GOON I, II, III & IV
BRED BY THE SLUMS I, II, III
BLAST FOR ME I & II
ROTTEN TO THE CORE I II III
A BRONX TALE I, II, III
DUFFLE BAG CARTEL I II III IV V VI
HEARTLESS GOON I II III IV V
A SAVAGE DOPEBOY I II
DRUG LORDS I II III
CUTTHROAT MAFIA I II
KING OF THE TRENCHES
By **Ghost**

LAY IT DOWN I & II
LAST OF A DYING BREED I II
BLOOD STAINS OF A SHOTTA I & II III
By **Jamaica**

LOYAL TO THE GAME I II III
LIFE OF SIN I, II III
By **TJ & Jelissa**

IF LOVING HIM IS WRONG…I & II
LOVE ME EVEN WHEN IT HURTS I II III
By **Jelissa**

PUSH IT TO THE LIMIT
By **Bre' Hayes**

BLOODY COMMAS I & II
SKI MASK CARTEL I, II & III
KING OF NEW YORK I II, III IV V
RISE TO POWER I II III
COKE KINGS I II III IV V
BORN HEARTLESS I II III IV
KING OF THE TRAP I II
By **T.J. Edwards**

WHEN THE STREETS CLAP BACK I & II III
THE HEART OF A SAVAGE I II III IV
MONEY MAFIA I II
LOYAL TO THE SOIL I II III
By **Jibril Williams**

A DISTINGUISHED THUG STOLE MY HEART I II & III
LOVE SHOULDN'T HURT I II III IV
RENEGADE BOYS 1-4
PAID IN KARMA 1-3
SAVAGE STORMS 1-3
AN UNFORESEEN LOVE 1-3
BABY, I'M WINTERTIME COLD 1-3
A THUG'S STREET PRINCESS 1&2
By **Meesha**

A GANGSTER'S CODE 1-3
A GANGSTER'S SYN 1-3
THE SAVAGE LIFE 1-3
CHAINED TO THE STREETS 1-3
BLOOD ON THE MONEY 1-3
A GANGSTA'S PAIN 1-3
BEAUTIFUL LIES AND UGLY TRUTHS
CHURCH IN THESE STREETS
By **J-Blunt**

CUM FOR ME 1-8
An LDP Erotica Collaboration

CRIME PAYS 3 | SELF MADE TAY

BLOOD OF A BOSS 1-5
SHADOWS OF THE GAME
TRAP BASTARD
By **Askari**

THE STREETS BLEED MURDER 1-3
THE HEART OF A GANGSTA 1-3
By **Jerry Jackson**

WHEN A GOOD GIRL GOES BAD
By **Adrienne**

THE COST OF LOYALTY 1-3
By **Kweli**

BRIDE OF A HUSTLA 1-3
THE FETTI GIRLS 1-3
CORRUPTED BY A GANGSTA 1-4
BLINDED BY HIS LOVE
THE PRICE YOU PAY FOR LOVE 1-3
DOPE GIRL MAGIC 1-3
By **Destiny Skai**

A KINGPIN'S AMBITION
A KINGPIN'S AMBITION II
I MURDER FOR THE DOUGH
By **Ambitious**

TRUE SAVAGE 1-7
DOPE BOY MAGIC 1-3
MIDNIGHT CARTEL 1-3
CITY OF KINGZ 1&2
NIGHTMARE ON SILENT AVE
THE PLUG OF LIL MEXICO 1&2
CLASSIC CITY
By **Chris Green**

CRIME PAYS 3 | SELF MADE TAY

A GANGSTER'S REVENGE 1-4
THE BOSS MAN'S DAUGHTERS 1-5
A SAVAGE LOVE 1&2
BAE BELONGS TO ME 1&2
A HUSTLER'S DECEIT 1-3
WHAT BAD BITCHES DO 1-3
SOUL OF A MONSTER 1-3
KILL ZONE
A DOPE BOY'S QUEEN 1-3
TIL DEATH 1-3
IMMA DIE BOUT MINE 1-6
DYING FOR LIKES
By **Aryanna**

A DOPEBOY'S PRAYER
By **Eddie "Wolf" Lee**

THE KING CARTEL 1-3
By **Frank Gresham**

THESE NIGGAS AIN'T LOYAL 1-3
By **Nikki Tee**

GANGSTA SHYT 1-3
By **CATO**

THE ULTIMATE BETRAYAL
By **Phoenix**

BOSS'N UP 1-3
By **Royal Nicole**

I LOVE YOU TO DEATH
By **Destiny J**

I RIDE FOR MY HITTA
I STILL RIDE FOR MY HITTA
By **Misty Holt**

LOVE & CHASIN' PAPER
By **Qay Crockett**

TO DIE IN VAIN
SINS OF A HUSTLA
By **ASAD**

BROOKLYN HUSTLAZ
By **Boogsy Morina**

BROOKLYN ON LOCK 1 & 2
By **Sonovia**

GANGSTA CITY
By **Teddy Duke**

A DRUG KING AND HIS DIAMOND 1-3
A DOPEMAN'S RICHES
HER MAN, MINE'S TOO 1&2
CASH MONEY HO'S
THE WIFEY I USED TO BE 1&2
PRETTY GIRLS DO NASTY THINGS
By **Nicole Goosby**

LIPSTICK KILLAH 1-3
CRIME OF PASSION 1-3
FRIEND OR FOE 1-3
By **Mimi**

TRAPHOUSE KING 1-3
KINGPIN KILLAZ 1-3
STREET KINGS 1&2
PAID IN BLOOD 1&2
CARTEL KILLAZ 1-3
DOPE GODS 1&2
By **Hood Rich**

THE STREETS ARE CALLING
By **Duquie Wilson**

STEADY MOBBN' 1-3
THE STREETS STAINED MY SOUL 1-3
By **Marcellus Allen**

WHO SHOT YA 1-3
SON OF A DOPE FIEND 1-4
HEAVEN GOT A GHETTO 1&2
SKI MASK MONEY 1&2
By **Renta**

GORILLAZ IN THE BAY 1-4
TEARS OF A GANGSTA 1/&2
3X KRAZY 1&2
STRAIGHT BEAST MODE 1&2
By **DE'KARI**

TRIGGADALE 1-3
MURDA WAS THE CASE 1-3
By **Elijah R. Freeman**

SLAUGHTER GANG 1-3
RUTHLESS HEART 1-3
By **Willie Slaughter**

GOD BLESS THE TRAPPERS 1-3
THESE SCANDALOUS STREETS 1-3
FEAR MY GANGSTA 1-5
THESE STREETS DON'T LOVE NOBODY 1-2
BURY ME A G 1-5
A GANGSTA'S EMPIRE 1-4
THE DOPEMAN'S BODYGAURD 1&2
THE REALEST KILLAZ 1-3
THE LAST OF THE OGS 1-3
By **Tranay Adams**

MARRIED TO A BOSS 1-3
By **Destiny Skai & Chris Green**

KINGZ OF THE GAME 1-7
CRIME BOSS 1-4
By **Playa Ray**

FUK SHYT
By **Blakk Diamond**

DON'T F#CK WITH MY HEART 1&2
By **Linnea**

ADDICTED TO THE DRAMA 1-3
IN THE ARM OF HIS BOSS
By **Jamila**

LOYALTY AIN'T PROMISED 1&2
By **Keith Williams**

YAYO 1-4
A SHOOTER'S AMBITION 1&2
BRED IN THE GAME
By **S. Allen**

TRAP GOD 1-3
RICH $AVAGE 1-3
MONEY IN THE GRAVE 1-3
CARTEL MONEY 1&2
By **Martell Troublesome Bolden**

FOREVER GANGSTA 1&2
GLOCKS ON SATIN SHEETS 1&2
By **Adrian Dulan**

TOE TAGZ 1-4
LEVELS TO THIS SHYT 1&2
IT'S JUST ME AND YOU
By **Ah'Million**

CRIME PAYS 3 | SELF MADE TAY

KINGPIN DREAMS 1-3
RAN OFF ON DA PLUG
By **Paper Boi Rari**

THE STREETS MADE ME 1-3
By **Larry D. Wright**

CONFESSIONS OF A GANGSTA 1-4
CONFESSIONS OF A JACKBOY 1-3
CONFESSIONS OF A HITMAN
CONFESSIONS OF A DOPE BOY
By **Nicholas Lock**

I'M NOTHING WITHOUT HIS LOVE
SINS OF A THUG
TO THE THUG I LOVED BEFORE
A GANGSTA SAVED XMAS
IN A HUSTLER I TRUST
By **Monet Dragun**

QUIET MONEY 1-3
THUG LIFE 1-3
EXTENDED CLIP 1&2
A GANGSTA'S PARADISE
By **Trai'Quan**

CAUGHT UP IN THE LIFE 1-3
THE STREETS NEVER LET GO 1-3
By **Robert Baptiste**

NEW TO THE GAME 1-3
MONEY, MURDER & MEMORIES 1-3
By **Malik D. Rice**

CREAM 2-3
THE STREETS WILL TALK
By **Yolanda Moore**

THE STREETS WILL NEVER CLOSE 1-3
By **K'ajji**

LIFE OF A SAVAGE 1-4
A GANGSTA'S QUR'AN 1-4
MURDA SEASON 1-3
GANGLAND CARTEL 1-3
CHI'RAQ GANGSTAS 1-4
KILLERS ON ELM STREET 1-3
JACK BOYZ N DA BRONX 1-3
A DOPEBOY'S DREAM 1-3
JACK BOYS VS DOPE BOYS 1-3
COKE GIRLZ
COKE BOYS
SOSA GANG 1&2
BRONX SAVAGES
BODYMORE KINGPINS
BLOOD OF A GOON
By **Romell Tukes**

CONCRETE KILLA 1-3
VICIOUS LOYALTY 1-3
BLOODY MONEY BAGS
By **Kingpen**

THE ULTIMATE SACRIFICE 1-6
KHADIFI
IF YOU CROSS ME ONCE 1-3
ANGEL 1-4
IN THE BLINK OF AN EYE
By **Anthony Fields**

THE LIFE OF A HOOD STAR
By **Ca$h & Rashia Wilson**

NIGHTMARES OF A HUSTLA 1-3
BLOOD AND GAMES 1&2
By **King Dream**

GHOST MOB
By **Stilloan Robinson**

HARD AND RUTHLESS 1&2
MOB TOWN 251
THE BILLIONAIRE BENTLEYS 1-3
REAL G'S MOVE IN SILENCE
By **Von Diesel**

MOB TIES 1-7
SOUL OF A HUSTLER, HEART OF A KILLER 1-3
GORILLAZ IN THE TRENCHES
OOPS CRY TOO 1&2
THE DAUGHTER OF A CARTEL BOSS
By **SayNoMore**

BODYMORE MURDERLAND 1-3
THE BIRTH OF A GANGSTER 1-4
By **Delmont Player**

FOR THE LOVE OF A BOSS 1&2
By **C. D. Blue**

KILLA KOUNTY 1-5
TENDER
By **Khufu**

MOBBED UP 1-4
THE BRICK MAN 1-5
THE COCAINE PRINCESS 1-10
STEPPERS 1-3
SUPER GREMLIN 1-4
A GANGSTA'S SON
By **King Rio**

MONEY GAME 1&2
By **Smoove Dolla**

CRIME PAYS 3 | SELF MADE TAY

A GANGSTA'S KARMA 1-5
By **FLAME**

KING OF THE TRENCHES 1-3
By **GHOST & TRANAY ADAMS**

BAD BITCHES WIT GUNZ 1&2
PROBLEM SOLVED
By **"Christopher Diesel" Hornezes**

QUEEN OF THE ZOO 1&2
By **Black Migo**

GRIMEY WAYS 1-3
BETRAYAL OF A G
By **Ray Vinci**

XMAS WITH AN ATL SHOOTER
By **Ca$h & Destiny Skai**

KING KILLA 1&2
By **Vincent "Vitto" Holloway**

BETRAYAL OF A THUG 1&2
By **Fre$h**

COUNTDOWN OF A KILLA 1&2
SEX, MURDER AND GOD 1&2
GUNS DOWN, BOTTOMS UP 1&2
By **Lo-Life**

THE MURDER QUEENS 1-7
By **Michael Gallon**

FOR THE LOVE OF BLOOD 1-4
By **Jamel Mitchell**

CRIME PAYS 3 | SELF MADE TAY

HOOD CONSIGLIERE 1&2
NO TIME FOR ERROR
By **Keese**

PROTÉGÉ OF A LEGEND 1,2&3
LOVE IN THE TRENCHES 1&2
By **Corey Robinson**

THE PLUG'S RUTHLESS DAUGHTER 1&2
By **Tony Daniels**

BORN IN THE GRAVE 1-3
CRIME PAYS
By **Self Made Tay**

MOAN IN MY MOUTH
By **XTASY**

TORN BETWEEN A GANGSTER AND A GENTLEMAN
By **J-BLUNT & Miss Kim**

LOYALTY IS EVERYTHING 1-3
CITY OF SMOKE 1-3
By **Molotti**

HERE TODAY GONE TOMORROW 1&2
By **Fly Rock**

WOMEN LIE MEN LIE 1-4
FIFTY SHADES OF SNOW 1-3
STACK BEFORE YOU SPLURGE
GIRLS FALL LIKE DOMINOES
NAÏVE TO THE STREETS
By **ROY MILLIGAN**

PILLOW PRINCESS
By **S. Hawkins**

CRIME PAYS 3 | SELF MADE TAY

THE BUTTERFLY MAFIA 1-3
SALUTE MY SAVAGERY 1&2
By **Fumiya Payne**

THE LANE 1&2
By Ken-Ken Spence

THE PUSSY TRAP 1-5
By **Nene Capri**

DIRTY DNA
By **Blaque**

SANCTIFIED AND HORNY
by **XTASY**

BOOKS BY LDP'S CEO, CA$H

TRUST IN NO MAN
TRUST IN NO MAN 2
TRUST IN NO MAN 3
BONDED BY BLOOD
SHORTY GOT A THUG
THUGS CRY
THUGS CRY 2
THUGS CRY 3
TRUST NO BITCH
TRUST NO BITCH 2
TRUST NO BITCH 3
TIL MY CASKET DROPS
RESTRAINING ORDER
RESTRAINING ORDER 2
IN LOVE WITH A CONVICT
LIFE OF A HOOD STAR
XMAS WITH AN ATL SHOOTER